About The Author

Joan M Moules is the author of over thirty books both fiction and non-fiction.

She also writes short stories and articles, runs occasional day workshops and is passionate about her writing. In junior school her desk was next to a window which looked across to a railway line and she was always in trouble for gazing across to the trains and making up stories about where the people on them were going instead of concentrating on what the teacher was saying. Eventually she was moved to the other side of the room where she couldn't see them... Some of her other interests, not in any special order, include reading, walking by the seashore, theatre, music hall, Victorian and Edwardian jewellery, cats and being with her family and friends. She is a member of The Society of Women Writers' and Journalists, Society of Authors, The Crime Writers Association and The Deadly Dames.

ISBN 9781912582273

Williams & Whiting (Publishers)

15 Chestnut Grove, Hurstpierpoint,

West Sussex, BN6 9SS

For Connie and Michael

who first introduced me to Venice

VENETIAN MAGIC

Joan M Moules

Williams & Whiting

CHAPTER 1

Cathy gazed unseeingly through the window of the train taking them to Dover. It still seemed incredible that she was here, sitting in a first class carriage opposite a sleeping Aunt Mary, on the first step of a journey to Venice. Sighing softly she turned her head to look across at her silent companion. Mary Fielding's blue eyes were closed, her vital face relaxed in slumber as the train rushed through the English countryside.

Closing her own eyes Cathy let her thoughts wander over the sudden turn of events. This time last week she had felt utterly miserable – the parting from Steve, loss of her job, it was as though everything bad was being thrown at once. Then, out of the blue came the chance of this job with her aunt. She realised now that her mother had told her sister Mary of the disasters that had fallen thick and fast, and it could not have worked better from Aunt Mary's point of view. Her own secretary, Pippa, who had been with her for years, had suffered a slight heart attack and been advised to rest, for six months at least, and Aunt Mary had taken on a temp who, at almost the last moment, refused to leave England for Italy, 'or for anywhere come to that.'

'Had just got her into my ways too. The first month she was practically useless,' her aunt had said. Cathy did laugh then, for she knew how fast her novelist aunt's mind worked, and how illogically sometimes. Pippa had been used to the rapid dictation, the sudden silence, and then another grand outpouring. 'In fact,' Mary often said,

'I really believe Pippa could write the romances better than me, she is marvellous at supplying the right word when needed, and bridging the gaps between scenes.'

The girl who wouldn't go to Venice had cared enough to recommend someone else. 'A friend of mine who is reliable and used to authors,' she told Mary.

Mary Fielding had interviewed Lyn, the friend, and feeling satisfied that she would do a good job until Pippa could return, had engaged her. It was the sheerest bad luck on her part, and good luck on Cathy's, that the girl had been involved in an accident a few days before their departure. A broken arm and various other minor injuries prevented her from being of any further use to a writer who needed an able bodied secretary.

When Aunt Mary had offered Cathy the job, 'You'll have to work mind, but the social life is good too. I'll introduce you around,' she said, Cathy hadn't hesitated. Her shorthand speed was good, her typing excellent, and without boasting she knew she could handle most people who might be annoying to a celebrity. Dear Aunt Mary, she worked hard and wrote books which were translated into many languages and which sold well. She signed autographs, chatted to the fans who gathered round when they discovered who she was, and always with a charming and faintly surprised air which suggested she wasn't quite sure what the fuss was about.

'I enjoy my little romances,' she told Cathy, 'but I would really like to do a thriller. Gave my editor a shock when I broached the subject once. 'You stick to romance

Mary,' he said to me, 'that's what your readers want from you – don't disappoint them.'

The woman in the corner stirred but did not wake, and Cathy opened her own eyes and, taking her compact from her bag, checked her makeup. The eyes that looked back at her from the tiny mirror were wide and long lashed, almost green Steve used to say. She smiled grimly at her reflection, and moving her head slightly, pushed the deep chestnut curls back over her shoulder. Maybe she should have had her hair cut as she was travelling to a hot country, yet there really had not been time to think about it. From the moment Aunt Mary telephoned to ask if she would like a job for six months, life had been a mad rush.

Her passport was in order, and living at home with her widowed mother she hadn't needed to worry about household arrangements, yet the two days before they left were filled with activity. Between ringing up some of her friends with the news that she would be out of the country for a few months, she managed to go into town and buy what she hoped were suitable clothes for Italy in April.

Italy was new territory for her; France and Germany she had visited, but Italy, and especially Venice, was a place she had long hoped to see. With a deft movement she closed her compact and returned it to her handbag, then turning once more towards the window she let her thoughts drift. She had gone a little mad, drawing deeply on sparse savings, and was pleased with her purchases.

Aunt Mary had an apartment bordering the Grand Canal, and although she worked hard during the day, Cathy knew she entertained lavishly in the evenings. As her niece as well as her temporary secretary, Cathy wanted to do justice to her aunt's hospitality.

Mary Fielding woke shortly before the train drew into Dover station. 'I wasn't much of a companion for you,' she said, smiling ruefully at Cathy. 'I don't usually sleep like that on journeys – I guess the trauma of these last few days have taken their toll. Must be getting old.'

Cathy leaned across and patted her aunt's plump hands. 'You don't look a day over fifty,' she told her, knowing that Aunt Mary was actually sixty three.

'Go on with you girl – not a day over sixty more like.' She looked pleased just the same.

At Dover they boarded the ferry. Aunt Mary had sent most of her luggage ahead of her, but Cathy had two bulging suitcases. The tall, dark haired man who handed her his small leather case and picked up her own heavy ones introduced himself when they were sorted out and comfortably seated. 'Grant Taggart,' he said briefly, 'on my way to Venice.'

'That's where we are going,' she answered. 'I'm Cathy Maddoc and this is my aunt, Mrs Mary Fielding.'

He lowered his head as he shook hands with Mary. 'Not the Mary Fielding?' he said softly, then, raising his eyes to look at her, 'but of course, I've seen you on television, and my mother never misses reading your latest book. I'll confess, Mrs Fielding, that I've not sampled one myself, but I know how much enjoyment they give to so many people, my own family amongst them. Thank you.'

Her clear blue eyes looked straight into his brown ones. 'It's very flattering to be recognised by a member of the younger generation, especially a male one.' She smiled at Cathy. 'If you wish to explore the ship my dear, go ahead; I have an interesting book in my bag and I plan to spend this short voyage dipping into that.' She reached into her travelling bag and Cathy laughed softly when she saw the title of the paperback she withdrew – *To Catch a Thief*.

'If I may offer my services as a guide, Miss Maddoc – Cathy,' he added, looking at her speculatively as she smiled at him. 'There isn't a lot, it's not like a cruise ship, but I would be happy to show you around. May we fetch you a drink, Mrs Fielding, before we go on our voyage of discovery?'

Mary murmured assent, and having left her settled comfortably with a martini and her detective novel, Cathy and Grant Taggart wandered away together.

'I usually travel by plane,' he told her, 'I've never made the journey by boat and train before. I'm researching for a book and I aim to be thorough.'

'But how interesting,' she said, 'what sort of books do you write?'

'Oh this is my first. That's why I didn't say anything about it in front of your aunt. I felt quite devastated when I realised who she was.'

Cathy laughed, and he caught her hand. 'Well, it's a new thing for me. We all know our own business best, and I'm very much a novice at this novel writing lark, whereas she…' he let her hand go and raised his upwards.

'I do see what you mean,' Cathy said earnestly, 'but she'd have been tickled pink to find a fellow author, whether it's your first or your hundredth effort. She's like that is Aunt Mary. She would simply have been very interested.'

'Have you been her secretary long?'

'No, only…' Cathy stopped speaking abruptly and gazed at her companion. 'What makes you think I'm her secretary?'

They had wandered towards the rail, and leaning on it now and looking down into the water he said quietly, 'The way you took charge I think. Although you introduced her as your aunt it was with the air of a secretary, if you see what I mean.' He turned to look at her. 'I'm sorry. Was I wrong? I – I didn't mean to offend.'

She smiled at him. 'You haven't. I was taken by surprise that's all. As a matter of fact I am going to be her secretary.'

By the time she returned to her aunt's side she knew that Grant Taggart was a much travelled man, had tried several careers, but was, as he put it, 'a bit of a loner.' His efforts into freelance journalism gave him the ambition to embark on a novel.

'I did a lot of travel articles, but these days so many periodicals and papers have their own travel correspondent,' he said, 'and I have always wanted to write a book..'

Cathy knew better than to ask what it was about at this stage. She was sufficiently close to her aunt to know that most authors preferred to talk of their brainchild after completion rather than while in progress.

Without mentioning Steve she told Grant about her unemployment and the chance of this temporary job in Venice.

'Aunt Mary and I have always been friends, and one of the places I long to visit is Venice.'

'Sometimes these things are providential,' Grant replied, 'you being out of a job for instance, so you were free to take this opportunity.'

'You're right. Aunt Mary has had the apartment here for some years now, but it's the first time I've been over and I am looking forward to seeing the sights.'

'I know Venice well. She is a beautiful city and I hope you will allow me the pleasure of showing her to you?'

'Thank you, Grant. I shall be working of course, but there will be free time too.'

'Write your address and telephone number down for me,' he said, producing a small notepad and pencil from his pocket, 'and I'll be in touch within a few days.'

Grant helped with the luggage when the boat docked, but did not sit with them in the train, although he looked in several times on the journey from Calais to Venice, and was on the platform when they changed trains at Milan, offering to buy a snack or drink to take back for the remainder of the journey.

'We shall have a meal on the train,' Mary said, 'but thank you for the thought, Grant.'

'He's rather nice, isn't he?' Cathy said later, as the train swayed its way through the Italian countryside.

'Yes.'

'You don't sound too sure, Aunt Mary.'

Mary looked thoughtful. 'I can't quite place him,' she answered slowly. 'What does he do? Is he an actor?'

'No, a writer. He's working on his first book.'

'How does he live meanwhile?'

Cathy confessed that she didn't know. 'He has done a variety of jobs, including freelance journalism, so maybe he has enough to live on for a while.'

They played chess with a travelling set Aunt Mary had brought with her, read their books and talked during the journey. When the train pulled into Venice station Grant was again on hand, and Mary smilingly thanked him for his help. 'We have friends meeting us, but I hope we shall see you during your own stay in Venice.'

'I too hope so. Au revoir, Mrs. Fielding. Cathy, I will telephone you in two days when you have settled in.'

As Cathy turned back from Grant's imposing figure Mary was affectionately greeting a short grey haired lady and the distinguished looking man with her. After she had kissed them both she introduced Cathy.

'My niece, who is going to be my secretary until Pippa returns. Cathy, meet two of my dearest friends, Betty and Guy Underwood.'

'Your first visit?' asked Guy, as he took charge of her cases while Mary walked on ahead with Betty.

'Yes, it is.'

'Well I hope you won't be disappointed that I haven't met you in a gondola. We run a little motor launch, which, while it isn't as romantic looking as a gondola, is certainly practical.'

Betty and Guy took them along the Grand Canal to Mary's home, extracting a promise from them to come along for a meal in about an hour to an hour and a half.

'No rush. When you have unpacked and relaxed,' Betty said, 'it will save you bothering tonight, and give us a chance to catch up with the London gossip.'

Cathy was thrilled with the atmosphere of Venice from the moment she walked down the steps of the station to stand on the banks of the Grand Canal. The steps and the immediate waterfront were cluttered with pigeons, but there before her was Venice, and for the first time in weeks she felt an excitement stirring in her veins.

The canal traffic was busy, motorboats and gondolas making a contrast with each other and with the ancient and modern aspects of the city. Everywhere it seemed there were flowers; they tumbled down terraces and balanced on balconies. As the boat moved through the water she didn't know which side of the canal to watch. Some of the buildings were shabby and some were splendid, and she glimpsed tantalising alleyways, shops, art galleries and museums.

The boats on the canal hooted noisily as Cathy, oblivious to the conversation around her, gazed at the panorama, at the sights and sounds, but especially the colours of Venice, the peach, terra cotta, the soft pinks and browns glowing in the romantic Venetian light.

It did not seem far to Mary's place. Guy pulled in by the landing stage, resplendent with red and white 'barbers sign' poles. He helped them both out, and then once more took Cathy's cases, carrying them into the dark entrance hall of the flat that was to be her home for the next few months.

'Thank you, Guy, see you later,' Mary said when he kissed her and raised his hand in a farewell salute to Cathy.

'Whenever you're ready, nice to have you back again.'

They travelled in the lift to the apartment where Ginette the housekeeper was waiting to greet them.

'I heard the launch and knew it must be you, Signora. Welcome, welcome, it is good to see you. I have the kettle on,' she added, beaming at her employer.

Mary kissed the dark eyed little woman on both cheeks. 'Thank you, Ginette. This is my niece, Cathy Maddoc. She will be my secretary until Pippa returns.'

'Ah, Pippa,' Ginette echoed sadly when she had shaken Cathy's hand, 'how is Pippa?'

'Doing very well, Ginette. She sends you warmest regards, and I have in my bag a little note for you from her.'

'Ah Signora. I will go now and make you what Pippa calls your "inevitable cup of tea."' Her voice hesitated over inevitable, dividing it into three words and sounding the second I as an e. You will tell Pippa I have mastered the word, Signora.' She went through one of the doors calling over her shoulder, 'I will have you unpacked very quickly, but for now the tea.'

Cathy followed her aunt into a spacious room with a balcony which overlooked the canal.

'Venice. It has a special magic for me, Cathy. It's not just all the loveliness out there,' she released the catch on the windows and stepped out onto the balcony. Tom and I spent our honeymoon here. Later, when we could afford it we came again, many times before he died as you know. Afterwards I thought I would not be able to bear to come again ever – yet it pulled me so much, and when, that first time I returned without him, I found the – the comfort that was here for me...' she half turned towards Cathy, 'but you don't want to listen to my old memories. Come along, I'll show you your room and the rest of the apartment. There is very little in the entrance as you probably noticed, because when the floods come the hall and basement suffer.'

She led the way back into the passage from which there were several doors. Flinging them open one by one she showed Cathy a panelled dining room, an extremely modern kitchen where Ginette was busy making tea, and a cool, blue tiled bathroom.

'The lift only comes as far as this floor. It's stairs then to reach the bedrooms.'

There were three, and a very tiny extra bathroom. 'In England I suppose it would have been called the box room,' Mary said, 'but the people I bought the flat from had modernised it.'

'It's lovely Aunt Mary,' Cathy said as she gazed around. Her bedroom and her aunts overlooked the canal. The spare one overlooked a small piazza.

11

'Not a noisy one,' Mary told her, 'although there is a café there which is busy during the day, but is not a haunt of tourists by night. They mostly go for the larger piazzas. Now, shall we have a cup of tea then we can unwind and rest a little before we go to Betty and Guy's for a meal. How kind that is of them. They are dear people and I see quite a lot of them when I am here.'

They drank their tea on the balcony where it was cool and pleasant in the early evening light, and Cathy asked about the routine and venue of the work.

'Yes, we didn't have much time to discuss this sort of thing beforehand, did we?' Mary said. 'I work in the dining room in the mornings, and here in the drawing room after lunch. I don't take the siesta which is common here – it breaks my train of thought too much, and it's perfectly easy to continue with the blinds down to keep out the sun. I usually stop between four and five, and from then until ten o clock the next morning you are free. Saturdays and Sundays I shan't require you. Often I do work then, but not dictation. The morning session usually finishes about twelve, and Pippa often typed a lot of it up between then and lunch at one, and finished it before ten the following morning. I don't need to see it daily, but I like the weeks work typed ready for me to go through at weekends.'

Cathy found that Ginette had unpacked and stored her clothes in the wardrobe and twin white chests of drawers in her room. The pink washbasin toned in with the pale pink walls and the beige and pink curtains and covers. She washed and changed into a cool cotton dress, brushed her naturally wavy hair until the copper tints glowed, then ran down the stairs to wait in the drawing room for her aunt.

Betty and Guy's flat was a few yards along from Mary's. They went through the other entrance which led onto the small piazza Cathy had seen from the spare bedroom window. An appetising aroma greeted them as they followed Guy up the marble staircase.

'We haven't been modernised as Mary has,' he apologised laughingly to Cathy, 'no lifts here I'm afraid.'

Betty came forward to greet them with hugs and kisses and Guy said, 'This is Scott, our nephew.'

A tall man with honey coloured hair rose from a chair near the window and came forward, hand outstretched. 'How do you do.'

They all had drinks on the veranda, then into the sumptuous dining room for a delicious meal starting with pasta, going onto fish and salad, and finishing with various kinds of cheese. Scott, who was next to Cathy at the table asked, 'Did Guy say you were Mary's niece?'

'That's right.'

'I thought she was bringing her secretary with her?'

Cathy looked at him. 'I am her secretary also.'

For a moment he seemed quite shaken, then he smiled at her and she noticed his brown eyes and thought what an interesting combination it was – rich dark eyes and golden hair.

'Temporary perhaps?'

'No, I shall be with her all the while she is here.'

Guy, sitting the other side, spoke to her before Scott could reply, but she was conscious of the rather wary looks he seemed to be giving her from time to time. When they left the table and went into the other room for coffee Betty said, 'Cathy I'm sure you will love Venice. When Mary lets you off work do pop along and see us anytime, you will be most welcome. I'm sorry for the girl who broke her arm, but it will give you six months in one of the most interesting places in the world, won't it?'

Aware of Scott's venomous look, Cathy agreed. He pulled her back slightly as they went downstairs to leave a little later. 'Why did you let me think you were the proper secretary,' he hissed. Taken aback she jerked his arm from hers.

'Why?' he insisted. 'Did you know the girl who was coming – the one who broke her arm?'

'What has that to do with you,' she said rather more sharply than she intended.

'More than you think. Listen, we must meet. Can you get off for coffee tomorrow morning?'

'Of course not.'

They had reached the bottom of the stairs and further private conversation was impossible. As they went through the door he called to her, 'Cathy, I'll 'phone you tomorrow then,' and because she didn't want to offend either her aunt or their hosts she raised her hand in a wave to them all, but did not answer him.

CHAPTER 2

Cathy slept well, and woke next morning to the sounds of the canal traffic. For a moment she forgot where she was and wondered what the hooting she could hear was about. Slowly she stretched and smiled to herself. Of course, below her window the hustle of working life was going on.

Reaching out for her watch she saw with alarm that it was eight fifteen. Goodness, didn't Aunt Mary say last night that she usually breakfasted at eight thirty? She rushed to the small bathroom, emerging ten minutes later fresh and sparkling. Throwing off her cotton housecoat she dressed quickly and hurried downstairs. Mary was already seated at the table and greeted her niece with a smile.

'Sleep well, dear?'

'Yes thanks. Almost too well.' She laughed, 'I've only been up fifteen minutes. Must be the Venice air, or the wine last evening.'

'Buono Giorno, Signorina.' Ginette came quietly into the dining room with an ice cold jug of orange juice. The telephone rang as she set it on the table. 'Scusi.' She hurried to answer it, returning seconds later to say, 'It is for you Signorina Cathy. Signor Taggart on the telephono.'

The telephone was in the hall, and when Cathy returned five minutes later Mary said, with a laugh in her voice, 'He wasted no time.'

'He asked me to meet him this evening for a meal and a brief tour of Venice. Is that all right? You have no plans, Aunt Mary?'

'No plans dear, you go right ahead and make your arrangements. I should have warned you that I seldom work on the first day here, so you are free until tomorrow morning. It gives us both a chance to relax after the journey, sort things out and organise. I shall have a lazy morning, and visit friends late this afternoon I think. I imagine you will want to take a look at Venice. There is much to see but you have six months and I've never thought it a place you could rush around. It truly is a place to "stand and stare". How about if we meet for a drink and a bite to eat around lunchtime? Ginette cooks for us in the evening by the way, so any time you are going to be out please let her know.'

'If you're sure I can't help with anything Aunt Mary, of course I'd love to explore a little.'

'Fine. And you had better start calling me Mary I think, don't you? Not such a mouthful, and as we shall be working many hours together it will be easier. I'll show you where Harry's Bar is before you go, I've a map here.'

There was another telephone call for Cathy just before she left the apartment. This time it was Scott Underwood, and he too wanted to take her for a meal.

'Sorry but I'm already going out this evening.'

'Lunchtime then. You won't be working right through, will you?'

'I can't manage lunchtime,' she said, preparing to replace the receiver.

16

'When can I see you Cathy? It's very important.'

'I don't think I want-'

'Please Cathy, there's a lot at stake. I have to talk to you.' The urgency in his voice was unmistakable.

'Why all the mystery,' she said, 'you're talking to me now, so tell me whatever it is you want to say.'

There was an awkward little silence, and then Scott said evenly. 'I can't. Not over the 'phone. How about tomorrow evening? Believe me,' he rushed on, 'I do need to see you alone.'

Her aunt came downstairs at that point and went into the kitchen where Ginette was singing as she worked, and remembering that Scott was Mary's best friends nephew she said into the mouthpiece, 'Very well, I'll meet you tomorrow evening.'

'Thank you Cathy. I'll come for you at seven.' He rang off quickly and she stood for a moment with the receiver still in her hand. Perhaps he was afraid I might change my mind, she thought. I've never been so sought after before, first Grant, who seems rather dishy; now Scott, who appears to think he knows everything, but I'll see what he has to say, if only as a courtesy to Aunt Mary. Anyway he wasn't likely to be staying more than a couple of weeks.

Cathy went to Piazza San Marco first, and it was as magical for her as she had hoped it would be. She wandered round under the vast colonnades, admiring the beauty of the glass, the splendour of the gold and silver displayed in the shop windows. Listening to the multiplicity of languages around her she remembered her

17

history teacher once attempting to describe Venice to a class of boisterous twelve year olds.

"It is almost impossible to describe with words – you need to see it with your eyes and with your heart. Some of you may go there one day, and if you do, look at it all, not just San Marco and Doges Palace, but the smaller places too. The piazzas and the little bridges, the Venice where the people live as well as the one the travellers see…" She was to be here for six months, time to explore the untouristy parts of this city on the water as well as the travel brochure bits of it.

Six months – time also for her wounded pride to heal, for she knew, deep within herself that it was mostly her pride that had been so badly bruised when Steve told her it was over, that he had met someone else.

She had grown up with Steve. He wasn't exactly the boy next door, but the boy down the road, and from walking to school together they had progressed to teenage discos, and, on her eighteenth birthday, an unofficial declaration of love.

'Later on I'll buy you a ring, but for now you're my girl, aren't you, Cathy?' he had whispered urgently. Starry eyed, she had put her arms round him and told him yes, for ever and ever. All that seemed a long while ago now. They had both gone on to other relationships briefly, but on her twenty first birthday they came together again, and for the last two years she knew her mother and Steve's parents were hoping and expecting they would marry.

She had thought so herself and been happy at the prospect. When the blow fell – "Cathy, I'm in love with someone else," Steve said quietly and bluntly one evening, she was shattered. Too shattered to even lose her famous temper. That had happened a week later at work and had cost her her job.

'But Cathy, you mean you resigned and walked out just like that? What will you do, jobs aren't exactly easy to come by,' her mother argued.

Aunt Mary – she must get used to calling her Mary, hadn't questioned her at all when she offered her the chance of being her secretary for the six months she was in Venice.

'Pippa who has been with me for twenty years is off sick as you know,' she said, 'and the girl I've been training for a month has let me down, and her replacement is now in hospital. I know you're at a loose end temporarily Cathy,' she said, 'and I need a secretary for the six months I'm in Venice. Would the job appeal to you? I expect Pippa will be fit for work again by then.'

As easy as that. Now she intended to enjoy Venice, to see as much of the surrounding Italian countryside as possible, and maybe by the time she returned people would have forgotten about her and Steve, because she knew that hurt almost as much as him falling in love with someone else. Almost.

'Sorry,' she apologised as she bumped into a dark eyed Italian who gazed at her longingly.

'Signorina you are alone, and so beautiful…'

19

'Not alone,' she said quickly, 'meeting a signor,' and she hurried away and into a shop which had the most wonderful display of glass and ceramics in the window.

The morning went all too quickly. She did not try to take in the sights, there would be time for that later. At present she was more than content to drink in the beauty around her. She had promised to meet Mary at noon, and as she stood in the famous piazza and gazed towards the Basilica of St Marks she experienced a surge of wonder that she was here in this ageless city and about to start a new, exciting job, when only last week she had felt that life was passing her by. She was making her way to Harry's Bar in plenty of time to meet Mary when Scott's rich sounding voice reached her.

'Cathy, what a pleasant surprise. Have you time for a drink before you return to work?'

She turned round. 'Why Scott, you startled me. Actually I'm on my way for one. I'm meeting Mary in,' she glanced at her watch, 'in ten minutes.'

'Mind if I come along?' Without waiting for an answer he fell into step beside her. 'Been seeing the sights in your lunch hour?'

'No, I had the morning off.'

'I wish I'd known. We could have spent it together. You never mentioned that when I spoke to you on the 'phone earlier.'

Cathy felt her temper rising and made a visible effort to control it and appear calm. 'Actually I didn't know then.' Her angry feelings won as she added, 'and if I had, I suppose it wouldn't occur to you that I may not wish to spend the time in your company?'

'You are making it very obvious,' he said, 'so I will escort you to Harry's Bar, but not force my attentions on you beyond that. I take it that is where you are meeting your aunt?'

He took her silence for agreement and suddenly asked, 'By the way, how long have you known Grant Taggart?'

'That also is none of your business,' she answered icily.

They had reached Harry's Bar. 'Until tomorrow, Cathy. Arriverderci,' he said and before she had time to protest he walked away into the crowds.

Mary loomed up beside her. 'Hullo dear. Wasn't that Scott Underwood I saw talking to you just now?'

'Yes, it was.'

Mary looked at her nieces flushed face and said no more about Scott. 'Let's go in and mingle with the rich and famous. It's usually crowded in here this time of day, but fun. Afterwards, if you have no other plans of course, we'll have lunch in a trattoria I frequent often when I'm here. It is not in San Marco, you won't mind that, will you? The food is wonderful and you will see the real Venetians,' she added softly.

Cathy left her aunt after the excellent lunch. Mary was calling on friends, renewing contacts, and although she offered Cathy the chance to accompany her, the girl declined.

'You don't want me tagging along spoiling your reunions because I'm new to Venice,' she said, smiling, 'and I'd like to wander a little anyway. So far I've only seen St Mark's Square.'

She did wander. Through little streets and over dozens of little bridges which crossed the minor canals. Sometimes she stopped and visited a church where there were usually several beautiful paintings. Once or twice she thought she was lost and would probably still be wandering in the little streets trying to find her way out of the maze all night. Then she would see a sign pointing to San Marco or Acadamia, and she followed it until she reached her starting point again. From here she knew the way.

She wore one of her new dresses for her evening date with Grant. In moss green she knew it showed her lovely chestnut hair to advantage. With it she wore the pearls Steve had given her for her twenty first birthday, and when Grant said, with admiration in his voice, 'Cathy you are beautiful,' she felt that it was true.

They ate in a small trattoria in what seemed to her a little back street, but the cuisine was excellent and Grant was stimulating company. He told her about one of his jobs as a courier.

'Some of the questions the holidaymakers asked,' he gave a mock shudder, 'often made me wonder if it was as boring for them as it was for us?'

'But surely you wouldn't take on a job like that if you weren't interested in people and places Grant?'

'I was interested, but only for a limited time. The fault was probably mine. I've not the temperament to be a teacher to a lot of timewasters. And it wasn't earning me much anyway.'

He gazed intently at her across the small table, and his dark eyes seemed to become very gentle as he said softly, 'Why all this talk about me, Cathy? I want to know about you.'

She told him quite a lot. How she had been at a loose end so had taken the job offered her by her aunt. 'I have always wanted to see Venice,' she said, 'it seemed a good opportunity to see the place and earn while doing so.'

'A girl after my own heart. Well I shall be here for a while, all summer in fact, so I hope we shall see a lot of each other. Your Aunt sounds like a reasonable person – does she give you plenty of time off?'

'Enough,' Cathy replied, smiling at him across the table.

'I'll ring you tomorrow,' he said when he left her, 'when is the best time, the most convenient. I don't want to antagonise your aunt.'

'I start work at ten, so any time before then Grant.'

'Will do. Goodnight lovely Cathy.' He tilted her face upwards and kissed her lightly and expertly, 'Sleep well.'

Strangely she didn't, in spite of the sudden tiredness which came over her when she was ready for bed. The apartment was air conditioned, and although it was a very warm night for the time of year, she felt comfortable; yet sleep eluded her. Every time she closed her eyes she saw in her imagination Scott Underwood, angry as he had looked at lunchtime when she had spurned him. Yet he actually had the nerve after that, to still expect her to meet him tomorrow evening.

She thought of Grant Taggart and felt calmer. He at least behaved in a conventional manner. Scott's abrupt questioning made her face flame, even in retrospect. And how had he known Grant's name? Eventually she slept and in her dreams she saw both Scott and Grant, the one so dark and sophisticated, the other so fair and filmstarrish, and in spite of her misgivings and anger with Scott, in her dream she knew she was fascinated by him.

She was up early the following day, her first working day in Venice, and all her thoughts were concentrating on the tasks before her when she went down to breakfast. They were halfway through the meal when the bell rang and they heard Ginette tripping down the stairs to answer it. She returned a few moments later with an enormous bunch of roses.

'For you, signorina,' she said, handing Cathy an envelope, 'shall I put them in water for you while you finish your meal?'

'Yes please, thank you, Ginette.' Wonderingly she took the small envelope in her hand. 'Do you mind if I look?' she said to her aunt, adding quietly, 'what a lovely, romantic thing to do.'

Slitting the envelope open with a knife, she pulled out a card and tried to stifle the amazed gasp that escaped her lips. When she saw Mary watching her gently she said, 'I – I thought they must be from Grant, you know we went out last night?'

'And – they're not?' Mary questioned softly.

'No. They're from Scott.'

She laid the card on the table and they finished their breakfast, but when she went to the kitchen afterwards to look at the beautiful bowl of pink, red, and yellow roses Ginette had lovingly arranged, she remembered the words on his card. "With my apologies. May I have a second chance? Scott."

Her day was busy. Mary started dictating promptly at ten and finished at eleven thirty.

'That's it for this morning I think,' she said. 'It's always slow at the start of a book, when I'm into it more we seldom finish before twelve. See you at two thirty Cathy.'

Mary really got into her swing during the afternoon session and it was almost five when they finished. Cathy had a quick bath and wore again the green georgette dress because she had felt so good in it the previous evening. She especially needed to feel right because Scott was so antagonistic. Or was she the one at fault? She had snapped at him several times in their two meetings so far, yet what could he expect if he fired questions at her as though she were being interrogated.

He was undeniably handsome with that wonderful pale gold hair and broad physic, but in Cathy's book that was no excuse to be rude.

"Manners maketh man or woman" had been a favourite expression of her mother's when Cathy was growing up, and it had left an indelible impression. Scott Underwood might look and behave like the hero of an epic film, but in real life she wanted more than Adonis like looks and an authoritative manner.

Grant Taggart compared favourably against Scott in her estimation. Not quite as tall as the Underwood's nephew, yet he was not a small man and his dark complexion and attentive attitude already made her heart glow. He was fun, making her laugh, treating her as an intelligent human being, whereas so far Scott had been both patronising and arrogant. Well she would go out with him this evening and find out what it was that was so urgent yet could not be talked about on the telephone. She would try to keep her temper should he start firing questions at her again, because he was the nephew of her aunt's friends. 'But that is all,' she said to her reflection in the mirror, 'and if he starts being dictatorial again then I shall walk out of the restaurant, no matter who he is related to.' Or should it be 'to whom he is related' she asked herself, conscious of her new job as secretary to a writer.

Scott arrived promptly at seven, talked pleasantly with Mary for a few moments, and then turned to her, 'Shall we go?'

They went through the back door which led into the little square visible from the spare room window, and without preamble he said, 'I thought we'd go to a small restaurant I know where we can talk. It isn't far.'

Taking hold of her arm he tucked it into his, seemingly oblivious of the fact that already she was angry. It was the way he said and did things, she decided as she walked silently beside him. Taking it for granted that his choice would be the one to count.

'So this is your first time in Venice,' he said suddenly. 'Mine too. It's a mysterious city.'

'So far I've found it to be quite beautiful and not at all mysterious.'

He glanced at her. 'I never said it wasn't beautiful – I said it was mysterious, and in many ways it is.'

They had been walking for about five minutes now and reached a bridge over a small canal. Gently he pressed her arm as he stopped on the parapet. 'There are both elements in this little scene, Cathy,' he said quietly, 'look.'

Gazing around her at the tall buildings reflected in the water below, the softness of the half-moon's light making dancing patterns on the grey water, and the eeriness of seeming to be only the two of them abroad at that moment she answered, 'It's lovely. Like a painting, so peaceful.' As she said it they heard the sound of singing which grew in volume as they stood together to watch a gondola glide into view. Four people sat in it listening to the gondolier singing his heart out as he expertly steered his boat along and beneath the bridge. Swiftly they both turned to watch his progress until he was out of sight.

'The most expensive way to see Venice,' Scott said quietly.

'But very romantic.' She was aware her voice sounded defensive, but since their first meeting the other evening she had seemed to clash with everything he said.

'Are you a romantic, Cathy?' he asked now, and there was a hint of teasing in his voice.

'I can appreciate the romance of a scene like that.'

'And you think I do not?' His voice was low and his hand still on her arm.

Angrily she shook herself free, 'I don't care one way or the other, Scott. I came with you this evening because you said you had something urgent and important to say to me, and also a little because your relatives and mine are friends and I suppose I was trying to be courteous to them. Believe me I did not come out with you to be romantic – you don't appeal to me in that way.'

She felt her cheeks burning as she stopped, and he said, with no hint of amusement now in his voice, 'You are a little firebrand, aren't you? But you have nothing to fear from me, I have no desire to tame you Cathy. Now shall we go for a meal, and,' he raised his voice very slightly, 'and how about a truce for the next couple of hours, then maybe I can get through to you the fact that you could be in great danger from someone.'

CHAPTER 3

It was a grand meal – they both chose the fish and with it a delicious white wine. Strangely, when they reached the restaurant and ordered Scott refused to talk about the 'danger'. 'Let us enjoy our food, time enough when we have finished,' he said, and in spite of her anti feeling towards him Cathy was fascinated. What sort of man was it who could pester her so with the urgency to impart his knowledge of danger, and then deliberately talk of other subjects, 'so as not to spoil our eating.'

She learned that he was in Venice for longer than the week or two she had surmised. 'I can't tell you a lot Cathy,' he said, 'only that I shall remain here for as long as seems necessary.'

When they were replete he ordered coffee. 'I hate to break the spell,' he said, his brown eyes soft and dark as he looked across the table at her, 'but perhaps the time has come now to talk seriously Cathy.'

'I'm waiting Scott. Better make it good.'

An expression she couldn't fathom appeared for a second in those so expressive eyes, and as she realised how well they had been responding to each other for the past hour she felt ashamed of her flippancy.

'OK, that was uncalled for. Sorry. But it does seem to me that you are making drama out of nothing.'

He ignored her remark and after the waiter had served their coffee he continued. 'I am going to lay my cards on the table Cathy, because I believe you know nothing of the plot that was hatched before you became

29

your aunt's secretary. No, don't interrupt. For once will you just listen to what I'm going to say before you jump to conclusions?'

Her fair skin was slightly flushed, whether with anger or the wine and good food she didn't know, but with an exaggerated sigh she settled herself to hear him out.

'Your aunt I believe has never been a wildly extravagant woman with her money, but she loves jewels and has a fine collection. There is a gang which operates throughout the world and specialises in gems. They have the contacts and markets, and we believe their next victim is Mary Fielding. Now we know that she does not keep her valuables in the bank, that she likes to wear them, and it is feasible to expect the gang to know this also. We believe…'

'We – who is this "we"', she said, 'the police, the CID?'

'I am officially off duty, Cathy. I injured my arm some weeks ago, and although it has healed now the doctors say it isn't yet a hundred per cent, so I am on sick leave at present. I came here because of knowledge I picked up regarding the gangs next likely haul. Yes, Mary Fielding's collection.'

'So you are not here in an official capacity. Really you're playing detective, trying to pull off a big arrest on your own?'

'If you choose to think so by all means do. Just answer me one question now. Do you believe what I have been telling you?'

It seemed so far-fetched to Cathy – more like something from a novel or a film, yet…

'I don't know, Scott. I honestly don't know. If – if what you say is true, then how are they going to do it? How many of them are there? And do you know who they are?'

'The answer to all your questions is that I do not know,' he said, 'I wish I did. I only know the gang through their code names, and I wouldn't recognise one of them if they came and shook me by the hand. The secretary who came in at the last minute was in their employ I believe. It was bad luck for them when you came out instead of her, but I still think they will try for the jewellery.'

'Don't you think you ought to be telling my aunt this instead of me?'

'No. I don't want to make her nervy, and I do want to catch this gang. The fewer people who know the better.'

'But surely she is the one person who should be warned. Give her a chance at least to – to put them in the bank if she wished.'

'Do you think she would?'

'No.' They smiled at each other across the table. 'Actually I'm not convinced she has this marvellous collection. She does like rings and necklaces and she wears some beautiful items, but I don't know that she has that many, or what they are worth.'

'Then you'll just have to accept my word that she has, and that they are all valuable, and very marketable.'

Cathy didn't answer back quickly this time, instead she was visualising her aunt over the years, and, yes she did have some very lovely pieces, she recalled.

'I suppose I'm not much of a one for glitter and sparkle myself,' she said softly, 'so I didn't notice too much, but thinking back, I have seen her wearing some lovely necklaces and rings and, and things. I still think you should talk to her about this Scott. If what you say is true, then surely she, and the local police, should be warned.'

'And indirectly warn the gang too. Nothing would happen then. No, we have to catch them. Not a word of this conversation to anyone Cathy.'

'And if I do?' she countered, tilting her chin high.

Reaching across the table he gripped her hand fiercely, 'You mustn't. For everyone's sake. I want to catch the gang and I want no casualties among the bystanders.'

'You're hurting my hand,' she said, 'and if you want my co-operation it might be better if you asked instead of told. In any case I shall not make any promises. I haven't proof that you are trustworthy, or even that you are who you say you are.'

It didn't throw him a bit. 'Touché,' he said, releasing her hand, 'but I'm sure you can subtly enquire from your aunt, and also from my aunt and uncle as to who I am, what profession I'm in, and whether or not I am at present on sick leave. Shall we go?'

'You are conceited, ill-mannered, and – and – and I'll see myself home,' she cried as he signalled the waiter. Once more her hand was gripped so tightly that she could not free it. He walked round to her side of the table, effectively blocking her exit as he took out his wallet and paid the bill.

'They will think we are having a lovers tiff,' he said, smiling at her, but this time his eyes were serious, 'and they will take no notice if you struggle because the Italians are a romantic race. They are more likely to join in and surround us with encouragement, so if you want to see a full scale opera in this little restaurant, you are going the right way about it.'

When they were outside he said, 'Sorry Cathy, but you did rather ask for it you know.'

'Don't be patronising as well.' They walked back in silence, over the bridges, through the alleys, until they reached the square beneath Mary's flat.

'I'm truly sorry the evening finished this way Cathy.' He was standing very close, and for a moment she thought he was about to kiss her. She felt his hot breath on her cheek as she turned to go in. 'Goodnight Cathy.'

She walked away from him without replying. Mary was still up and called to her as she came in. 'Like a drink dear?'

'No thank you.' Then quickly she changed her mind. 'Yes, I will please.' She moved towards the tray on the side table, 'Shall I pour one for you?'

'Just a small refill.' Mary held out her glass, 'Did you have a nice evening?'

Cathy hesitated for a moment. The earnestness of Scott's warning echoed in her ears, yet every instinct told her to confide in her aunt. Would it seem like telling tales out of school? And Scott was Betty and Guy's nephew. She didn't have to like him, but she was bound to meet him sometimes during the time she was here, and she had no desire to cause ill feelings between her aunt and her friends.

'It was all right,' she said.

Mary's blue eyes twinkled. 'I had not met Scott until the other evening,' she said, 'although I had seen his picture and heard about him, but if I were thirty years younger and not the one man woman I am, I know he would have set my heart a flutter. There's something so honest to goodness about him.'

Cathy glanced at her aunt's fingers. She was wearing two rings this evening. One, her engagement ring, was a modest affair set with three small diamonds. The other was a large sapphire, it was truly beautiful and she found herself watching it as Mary picked up her sherry glass.

'I've been planning a few suppers this evening,' the older woman said, 'I think I told you I entertain a bit when I'm here. One of the joys of only living here for a limited time each year I suppose; you do get around to asking your friends to dine because you know you can't do it any time. Well this is what I've worked out for the next few weeks – Cathy, is there something wrong with my hand...'

Jerked out of her fascinated absorption Cathy coloured self-consciously.

'No. I'm sorry, I realise I was staring. I was admiring your ring.'

'Oh.' Mary laughed, 'I thought perhaps my hand had changed colour or something the way you were watching it.' She held her fingers out towards her niece. 'It's one of my favourites. Here, try it on, Cathy, although I think emeralds would suit you best. Especially with that lovely green dress. I've one that would complement it beautifully if you'd like to borrow it anytime.'

'I'd be much too nervous to wear something so expensive, but thank you for the thought.' She sipped her drink, 'Your necklace is beautiful too, like a night sky.'

'Tom and I bought this when I really began making money with my books. We were better off by then anyway, and when *The Brilliant Sapphire* became a bestseller we bought the ring and necklace. I had always loved good stones, not just glitter for glitters sake if you see what I mean, and this set was our celebration that after years of pegging away I had actually "made the charts" so to speak. Since then I've acquired quite a collection I suppose. Different pieces to suit different moods and colours. They have come from all over the world and I love them all, but the one that has such a special place in my heart, the one I wear every day, is this.'

She held her left hand towards Cathy. 'Your engagement ring,' the girl said, gently touching the ring on the third finger.

'Yes. We couldn't afford large stones, but these three caught our eye and we both liked them straight away. Probably the ring that is worth less than any other I have, but the one that means most to me. Hey, you'll have me sounding like the worst kind of romantic novel in a moment. And listen, I've just remembered, Grant Taggart, that chap we met on the journey here, telephoned. I told him you were out and I wasn't sure what time you would be in, so he said he would ring you early tomorrow morning.'

When they went upstairs to bed a short while later Mary said, 'Come and try this ring Cathy, while you still have that dress on.'

From a shelf in her wardrobe she took a large black leather jewel case, unlocked it with a small key from the keyring she kept in her handbag, and carried over to the bed a roll of soft brown velvet which, when unwrapped, revealed a miniature Aladdin's cave. Rubies, diamonds, opals, pearls, emeralds, gold and silver, some set in brooches, some in necklaces and ear-rings and pendants. There was a heavy gold bracelet, one or two lockets, and in the jewel box itself, wedged neatly into the black velvet slits, were the rings, fabulous enough to grace any jewellers shop window.

Cathy gasped aloud. 'But Mary, oughtn't you to keep all this in a bank vault?'

'Whatever for? Tom always said beauty was meant to be seen and enjoyed, not hidden away. When would I ever wear them if I kept them in the bank, or anywhere else reputedly safe?'

'You could get them out – the ones you wanted to wear when you were going anywhere special,' Cathy said quietly. But Mary was only half listening as she selected the emerald ring she had spoken of earlier.

'That would be a lot of trouble. I daresay I should never bother, and then no-one would have pleasure from them,' she answered, smiling at her niece. 'Oh I know what you are thinking – that I could be robbed. Well, believe it or not, Tom and I discussed all this years ago, and decided that while we would never leave them scattered over the dressing table, we would never become slaves to our possessions. Anyway, half the people who see them, and admire them even, never realise they are the real thing, there are so many good artificials on the market nowadays.' As she straightened up and handed a glittering emerald ring to Cathy, an image of a fair-haired, brown-eyed man came into the girls mind. A man who looked like the pictures of a Greek Adonis, and another image of the shadowy "gang" of which he had spoken, and she knew that there were more people in Venice who did know the true value of the jewellery than Aunt Mary thought.

'Go on, try it for size,' Mary said. It was slightly large, but the stone and the setting suited her hand very well, and, moving to the mirror Cathy spread her fingers across her breasts, to see the effect of the ring against her green dress.

'Yes, I understand what you mean about it,' she said slowly, turning back to her aunt, 'it does set it off and it feels positively luxurious.' Carefully she removed the ring and handed it back.

'We could get that one altered to fit you Cathy...'

'No, no you mustn't, it's yours.'

'One day it will be yours. There will be one or two pieces for friends, some for my two God-daughters, and the rest of it will be for you my dear. I see no reason why we shouldn't have that ring adjusted to fit you now. That way I too can enjoy seeing you wear it.'

Gently she replaced it in the box. 'I'll see about it while we are in Venice,' she said, 'now I think I'm for bed. It's so lovely to be here again and it always takes me a day or two simply savouring the joy of it I think, and renewing friendships, and then it is always as though I have never been away.'

Once again Cathy took a long time to sleep. The conversation with her aunt about the jewellery buzzed round and round in her head, and although she realised that Mary didn't show the collection to everyone, or even talk about it, she was extremely bothered by all Scott had told her. She wished she knew what to do. It was all very well for Scott Underwood to want a robbery to take place so that he could, presumably, catch the thieves red-handed, possibly winning kudos for himself, maybe even promotion, but she didn't relish the idea one jot. Prevention surely was the best method, and that would mean telling Mary of his suspicions and asking her to play safe and put the jewel box in the banks keeping.

She lay thinking about it all for a long while, then she remembered Grant's telephone call. While she obviously couldn't mention the subject to him or to anyone else, her spirits lifted as she thought about him. Tomorrow evening, if he asked her out again, promised to be more rewarding in terms of companionship than this one had been. Even so she woke in the early hours of the following morning with a dream still vivid in her mind, a dream where a tall, fair man was bending over her.

'I'm Scott Underwood,' he said, 'and I'm not asking, I'm telling you.' As he stooped to kiss her she woke up.

CHAPTER 4

They had been in Venice for two weeks when Mary Fielding threw a party. Cathy helped her draw up the list of guests.

'Betty, Guy, and Scott,' she said, 'The Fritters, June and Ray, Nigel and Barbara, and I believe they'll have her mother with them next Saturday, she's coming for a couple of weeks holiday, so put her down. Then Ted Cassy, Donald and Vi Cockington, Vanessa Silverton, oh and how about Grant Taggart – would you like him to be there, Cathy?'

The only names she knew amongst the long list Mary finished with were Grant's, Scott's, and Betty and Guy Underwood. She was amazed at how many English people there were living in Venice. 'Some, like me for only a few months,' Mary told her, 'but some, the Underwoods and Fritters for example, it is their permanent home, and they really only go to England for holidays or family visits sometimes.'

Cathy had been out with Grant several times since her arrival, and each occasion seemed better than the last. He had taken her for a trip in a gondola, and as the gondolier sang a barcarolle in a beautiful tenor voice, Grant's arm had stolen round her shoulders and for the first time since Steve left her she felt the stirrings of a deeper emotion.

Scott too had telephoned and invited her for a meal, and she was quiet and polite in her refusal. Always she made a reasonable excuse, which, when she thought about it seemed surprising to her, for it was more in her nature to say outright that she had no desire to go out with him. Yet she knew this wasn't quite true, there was a part of her that enjoyed the challenge of his antagonism. When she met him in the Mercuria where she was shopping for Mary two days before the party he suggested they have a cup of coffee together.

'I have to get back – ' she began to say, when he interrupted her. 'Cathy, I realise you want as little to do with me as possible, but I should like to talk to you. Would it hurt so much to sit at a table with me for ten minutes?' His voice was low, even a little teasing, yet his eyes regarded her seriously.

'Well Cathy? If I don't appeal, surely the lovely Italian cappuccino does.'

She smiled, surprised to discover how pleased she was at his gentle humour. 'Why not?' she said, equally lightly, 'I've finished my shopping and aren't on duty again for an hour.'

He took the shopping from her, 'Looks as though you've been busy,' he remarked, glancing at the full bag.

'Mostly bits and pieces for the party.'

'Ah yes, I've heard about your aunt's parties. They are quite famous here I believe. Will there be many people?'

'About thirty at the last count. How she will fit everyone in I don't know, but both Mary and Ginette keep assuring me that they will. Apparently she moves the furniture back against the walls, wedges the door open, and scatters cushions around the floor in both the lounge and hall, leaving the chairs for those who cannot get down low.'

'It sounds fun,' he said as the waiter came for their order. The coffee was delicious, and Scott, for once it seemed to her, not questioning and ordering, but simply being pleasantly social. They talked about England. He lived in Kent, he said, with his parents and younger sister, and like herself it was his first visit to Venice.

'And what do you think of it, Scott?'

'Magical. Magical and mysterious,' he said. She remembered the other evening and his insistence of the mystery of Venice, and she smiled to herself. Half an hour later he walked home with her, and as they talked about the paintings in some of the churches and at the Acadamia she began to wish he could always be like this instead of the bossy young man she had first met.

'Until the party,' he said as he returned her shopping bag to her outside the apartment.

'Yes. And thank you for the coffee, Scott.'

'Well it's good to know that we can get on with each other after all Cathy,' he replied quietly as he turned away.

She was in a thoughtful mood when she went indoors, and as there seemed to be no-one else about she unpacked the bag, stowing the goods away tidily in the kitchen before going to her room to prepare for the afternoon work session.

The party was to be held on a Saturday, and Mary, Cathy, and Ginette worked hard all the morning preparing tasty and attractive looking 'bits to nibble' as Mary called them, ready for the evening. Mary seemed to glow as the day wore on, and Cathy warmed even more to the woman she had always been so fond of. In the short while Cathy had been working for her aunt she realised how much she needed the stimulus of people. Not any people, 'not crowds just for the sake of crowds,' she said one night when they were talking over a late cup of coffee, 'but people who mean something to me – friends.'

Well, Mary seemed to have plenty of those, even out here away from her homeland, and although part of Cathy felt shy at meeting them all, another part of her was looking forward to it, because she thought they were likely to be interesting folk if they were connected with her aunt.

They all observed siesta in the afternoon on this occasion, and later Mary supervised the laying out of the food on the large table which had been moved against a wall.

Cathy was dressing when there was a light tap on her bedroom door. 'Who is it,' she called softly.

'Mary.'

'Come in, I'm almost ready.'

Mary looked very pretty in a pink cocktail dress with a full skirt. She had a clear, English rose complexion, and her face, framed by her white curly hair, was smiling now at her niece.

'I came to see what colour you were wearing. Oh that's lovely,' she said as Cathy held up the beige/gold dress which was lying on the bed. 'Have you already planned a necklace with it?'

'My pearls.'

'Mmm, they would be nice. If you'd like a change though, something different, you can borrow my amber. It would look well with that dress I think, don't you?'

Cathy laughed. 'You are determined for me to wear some of your lovely jewellery.'

'Not if you would prefer... it seems a pity not to share it, that's all,' Mary answered quietly as she turned away.

'I didn't mean it like that, it's just that I – well I'm afraid of losing or damaging your things...' Impulsively Cathy clasped her aunt's hands. Mary's blue eyes looked wistful as she said, 'I often wish I'd had a daughter. I've never said anything before, but you don't know how much I sometimes envied your mother.' Suddenly she was brisk again. 'Anyway, put your dress on, and if you want to try the necklace with it, pop into my room and do so. If not, no harm done.'

Cathy was thoughtful as she finished dressing. She brushed her hair until it shone like copper, then knocked on her aunt's door. 'I'd like to try the amber,' she said. It was exactly right, and even Cathy caught her breath for a moment as she looked in the mirror at the beautiful stones glowing against her creamy skin and reflecting the subtle golden tones of the dress.

'Well?'

'It's beautiful, Mary. I should love to borrow it for this evening.' Turning, she hugged her aunt, 'It is kind of you.'

'Nonsense. I shall have as much pleasure, maybe more, out of seeing them on you. You know that amber has healing qualities, don't you?'

'No.'

'It is reputedly good for chest and throat ailments, for rheumatism, and in olden days women wore it as a protection against witchcraft.'

Cathy fingered the almost golden amber beads around her neck. 'It is a very romantic sort of jewel,' she said, 'even its name, Amber, sounds dreamy.'

'There is a Greek tale that originally amber was the tears of Phaeton's sisters, who turned into trees as they wept for his death, but I like to think of its beauty and healing properties best.'

Cathy looked down at the necklace. 'It feels nice anyway,' she said, 'and I'm so looking forward to this party. You know since – since Steve and I broke up I haven't really been interested in socialising until now.'

Mary came and stood with her, 'and I'm looking forward to showing you off – you are looking beautiful, my dear.' She gave her a quick, sudden kiss, then, almost shyly she said, 'come on, let's check the kitchen.'

The first guests to arrive came by boat and Cathy watched from the veranda, and as she fingered the amber necklace she wore, and savoured the romance of Venice, she blessed her aunt for giving her this opportunity just when she was at a low peek in her life. Fleetingly she wondered what Steve was doing this evening, and she knew that if she had been with him she would have been content, but for how long? Since coming here she had experienced feelings for Grant Taggart that had never surfaced when she was with Steve, and this morning she had even liked Scott Underwood briefly.

Grant arrived on foot through the other entrance by the piazza, and as she introduced him to her aunt's friends, many of whom she herself had only just met, she was conscious of their appraisal of the two of them together.

The room filled up and people spilled out into the hall, and even the kitchen. Ginette circulated amongst them, offering dainty sandwiches, cocktail surprises, and drinks, and soon the place was a hive of chatter and laughter. She was deep in conversation with Grant when Scott arrived with his aunt and uncle. She saw and heard them but she didn't look up, and when Grant said, 'Who is that tall, fair haired bloke staring at you, Cathy?' she glanced round quickly, knowing he had been waiting for her to do just that.

'Scott Underwood,' she said, 'it's OK, Mary will see to them.' Then, remembering Scott's reference to Grant by name on only the second occasion she had met him she added, 'but you know him, don't you?'

Grant shook his head. 'No, certainly not by sight, and the name's unfamiliar. He's obviously English. Does he live here?'

'He's staying the summer with his aunt and uncle who are friends of Mary's.'

Grant laid his arm across her shoulder, 'I can see I'll have to watch out then. Keep your eyes in this direction, won't you Cathy?' His fingers played with the clasp on the back of her necklace. 'Those are very pretty beads, they suit you. Ah, here comes superman, heading in our direction.'

Cathy felt uncomfortable because Grant still had his arm round her, and she hastily scrambled to her feet.

'Hullo,' she said, including Guy and Betty in her smile, 'This is Grant Taggart. Grant, this is Betty, Guy and Scott Underwood.'

Introductions over they talked of Venice and the immediate area for a while, until Mary came to ask Betty and Guy to come and greet someone else, and they went off. Grant said, 'I'll see if I can help your aunt with the refreshments, shall I, Cathy? Leave her free to mingle with her guests. I won't be long. Don't go far.'

She gazed after him in amazement, and Scott said dryly, 'Getting his feet under the table, eh?'

Immediately she was indignant. 'What do you mean? It's a nice gesture on Grant's part. I should have noticed how busy she and Ginette are and suggested it myself. I'll go and help him,' but Scott put out a restraining hand.

'No, please stay and talk for a moment, Cathy. With all this crowd I might not have another chance to be alone with you.'

It would be churlish to refuse, she thought, yet her gaze wandered around trying to find Grant again.

'I don't believe you've listened to one word,' Scott said presently, 'and your precious Grant doesn't seem to be much in evidence with the sandwiches and drinks either.'

'That's a horrible remark to make, but one I should expect from you I suppose. You can't...' She was interrupted by Ginette, who beamed at them both as she proffered a large oval dish of canapés. 'Grant will be

46

round with more drinks in a moment,' she said, moving on to the next group.

'All right, don't say a word,' Scott whispered close to her ear, and she heard the laughter in his voice, 'he is helping and not snooping around the place as my nasty mind suspected for a moment.'

Before she could reply Mary was by her side. 'Cathy, can you come with me quickly for a moment?' she asked. 'Excuse us, Scott, but something has cropped up.'

Cathy followed her aunt through the throng and upstairs. 'Maria, whose baby isn't due until next month has started labour pains,' she explained as they went, 'will you stay and talk to her while I telephone for an ambulance? She's very scared.'

The woman sitting amongst the shawls and light coats on Mary's bed looked at them with dark eyes that were beautiful even in fright.

'Cathy will stay while I fetch the doctor,' Mary said, and hurried out again. Cathy sat beside the girl, for she was very young, and tried to reassure her that all would be well. Maria sat taut until another pain gripped her, when she hung on so tightly to Cathy's hands that they became numb. She had one more such pain before the doctor and ambulance arrived, and they walked down the stairs slowly and awkwardly, with Cathy holding her arm. They both went in the lift with her, and the curly headed husband whom Mary had quietly located on her return from the telephoning, and Cathy was amazed to find the ambulance was a motor launch. With the mother and

47

father-to-be safely installed in the boat Maria suddenly said, 'My handbag...'

'I'll see to it. Where is it, in the bedroom...' Mary's voice was soothing, and the boat chugged away from the mooring and Mary and Cathy returned to their guests. The party seemed to be well into its swing judging by the chatter as they stepped from the lift, and Cathy smiled to herself as she thought of the little drama they had just taken part in, while back here Grant and Scott and all the others were still sipping their drinks.

'I'll get Maria's handbag first, shall I?' Cathy said to Mary, 'and put it in my room, then it won't get mixed with any of the others.'

'And I'll mingle again and make sure everyone is all right in the other room. See you in a minute Cathy, and thanks for your help dear.' They parted in the hall and Cathy ran upstairs to her aunt's bedroom to find Maria's bag. The door was open and she was seized roughly and a hand thrust over her mouth as she entered.

'Cathy.' Scott's voice sounded utterly disbelieving, and in the reflected light from downstairs she could make out his tall figure and blonde hair.

'Let me go you beast,' she hissed, then crossing the room she switched on the light and confronted him. 'What do you think you are doing?'

'I was trying to catch someone who was prowling about up here.'

'A likely story,' she said. She looked at the wraps and bags scattered over the bed and Scott said quickly, 'Cathy,

I know this doesn't look good, but someone was up here a few moments ago and I was just too late.'

'Who was it?'

'I don't know. I have my suspicions but I don't know because I didn't see. But someone was after...' he moved over to her, 'your aunt's jewellery. This is her bedroom, isn't it? I don't think it was going to be stolen tonight, but I believe this was a reconnaissance.'

'That's ridiculous,' she said, 'why everyone here tonight is a friend of Mary's. Everyone is known to her.'

'Well I guess I was wrong then. I'm sorry I frightened you Cathy.'

'You didn't frighten me. Now I have a question to ask you. Who gave you authority to wander around like this? Does my aunt know you take it upon yourself to check other people's property?'

'I've said I'm sorry. As a matter of fact if you hadn't blundered up the stairs at that moment I *might* have caught whoever it was. I think he – or she – escaped into the bathroom as I came in, and when you arrived seconds later it gave them the chance to quietly slip back to the party.'

'Oh what a romancer you are. You should be in the writing business, Scott. Now I think we ought to rejoin the party, don't you? Otherwise someone else might come up to see if we are robbing the handbags!'

He switched the light off as they left the room, and followed her down the stairs where they parted company. Cathy, smiling at Grant, who was engaged in conversation with a small group in the corner, went towards her aunt who was talking to Betty and Guy Underwood.

'Ah Cathy, find it all right? I was just telling Betty and Guy about our excitement. I hope little Maria is doing well, the poor child was so nervous, but she has her husband with her, and probably by now most of his and her relations.'

'My goodness, no I didn't. I didn't even look for her handbag,' Cathy said. 'I –' she stopped, suddenly realising who she was talking to. 'I met someone on the stairs and never reached the bedroom at all. I'll go and fetch it now.'

'No Cathy, leave it. Stop and have a drink and enjoy the rest of the party. After all when everyone has gone, the bag that is left will obviously be Maria's,' Mary said, 'now stay right here and I'll fetch you something to eat and drink.'

While Mary was gone Betty and Guy asked her about Maria. 'Such excitement – to think the baby was almost born here.'

Mary not only brought food and drink with her, but also Scott. 'I have just been telling him about the little drama here this evening, and why I had to drag Cathy away from him so suddenly and rudely,' she said. 'Look I must go and mingle with the others. Help yourselves to more food, there's plenty in the kitchen.'

There was no chance for Cathy and Scott to talk privately together anymore during the rest of the evening, and Grant always seemed to have a crowd of people around him. She joined him several times, and he put his arm round her waist in a propriety fashion and carried on with whatever he was saying.

It was two o clock in the morning before the guests left, and Mary and Cathy rode back in the lift, helped Ginette to wash the glasses and plates, and then toiled wearily up the stairs to bed. Cathy took off the amber necklace and, tapping on Mary's door she went in quietly in answer to her aunt's invitation.

'Just to return your necklace,' she said. 'It is quite, quite beautiful, and wearing it has shown me a little of how you feel about your jewellery. It was a fabulous party, Mary, and I know now why your parties are so famous.'

'Well we did have extra drama tonight with Maria's baby. By the way I have rung the hospital and she had a son an hour ago. Both doing well.'

Cathy felt elated. 'That's wonderful, Mary. I'm so glad for her. For them both,' she added quickly. 'He seemed very nice, but shy and scared for her. Have they anywhere to live?'

'They are living with her parents – it's quite common in Italy. When a child marries they occupy part of the house, quite separate, and bring up their family. When the old people die they inherit the house and they, in their turn, have their youngsters in the other part of the house.'

'What if they have more than one child?' Cathy said.

'By the time the second one needs a roof the first have progressed to better things, and so on all down the line. Family life in Italy is very close.' Mary tried to stifle a yawn and Cathy said, 'I shouldn't think either of us will need rocking tonight. By the way did you find Maria's handbag, Mary?'

'Yes.' She indicated a wicker chair in the corner. 'I've put it over there and will take it to her tomorrow. Want to come, or have you a date with one of your beaus?'

Cathy paused and Mary laughed softly, 'I was only teasing dear, but it seems to me they are both keen.'

Keen for what, Cathy thought, when she was back in her own room and preparing for bed. While Grant seemed to like her as a person, Scott only wanted information that would lead to him catching these thieves he was so sure were operating in the area. Or was that an enormous cover-up for his real activities? If so, what were his real activities, and what was he doing in Mary's bedroom? Questions without answers seethed inside her head as she slipped between the cool sheets. Why had she lied when she went downstairs without Maria's handbag? If Scott had surprised someone up to no good in the room, who was it? In that half-light it would have been difficult to tell, although he had no trouble identifying her as soon as he touched her. In any case, she decided, she wasn't looking for a new man, except as an escort perhaps for the evenings. Nothing more. And of the two her aunt had been thinking about, Cathy knew with certainty which she would choose.

CHAPTER 5

Grant telephoned early on Sunday morning. 'It's a beautiful day, Cathy. How about us going somewhere together?'

'Fine. Give me an hour though, I've only just got up.' He was ringing the bell exactly one hour later.

'You're a good timekeeper, Grant,' she said, looking up at him, 'but you haven't caught me out. I'm ready.'

'Great. What would you like to do?'

'I'm in your hands,' she told him, 'you know the area far better than I do.'

'Fair enough. How about going to one of the islands. Burano is the one I think you'll like. Murano is the one where most of the glass is manufactured, but Burano and Torcello are easily accessible and we can do the two in a day. The steamers go from Burano to Torcello. How does that idea sound to you?'

'I can't wait.'

'Right. We'll get the steamer from the Fondamenta Nuove to Burano, which is like a baby Venice really, then later in the day we can visit Torcello, which has some magnificent old buildings. Are you interested in architecture?'

'Yes. I don't know a great deal about it, wish I did, but I am very interested.'

It was a beautiful sunny day, more like the middle of summer than spring, and as the steamer headed for the islands they looked back towards the skyline of Venice

53

and Cathy felt again that sense of wonder that so much had happened to her in less than a month.

She loved Burano immediately. The canals, the bridges, the houses and people. 'It is like a miniature Venice,' she exclaimed delightedly. They had lunch in a trattoria that was filled with good cooking smells and the excited chatter of people.

'You are easily pleased, aren't you, Cathy?' he said.

'I suppose so. I've not thought a great deal about it before, Grant. Don't forget I am only to be here for six months so I want to see as much as I can. This makes such a difference. If this was a permanent job I expect I would space things out more, but maybe not have as much enjoyment. As it is I'm looking on it as a sort of holiday.'

'Holiday in Venice,' he said, and his hand reached across the table for hers. 'It's a romantic setting and I hereby drink to your enjoyment of your six month sojourn in the Queen of the Adriatic. May you return again and again...'

Solemnly she raised her glass, 'Amen to that. Now it's your turn Grant. You haven't really told me very much about yourself at all, not even how long you will be here.'

'Haven't I? Well there isn't much to tell really, but if you're interested I'm thirty two, not married but have a healthy interest in girls, enjoy the good life, and by that I mean the rich life, but then who doesn't? What else? You know already that I've had umpteen jobs – I get bored with them quickly.'

'But not the book. You'll finish that, won't you?'

'Oh. Oh yes, I'll finish that.'

'How is it going?'

'Well to be perfectly honest with you I have not put pen to paper since my arrival.' His laugh rang out and he squeezed her hand, 'I haven't the dedication of your aunt, she has a set routine I suppose, that's how she manages such an output?' He leaned his elbows on the table, 'It fascinates me how other writers work, tell me about her, it might inspire me to stick more to a routine.'

She outlined their day and he said, 'Then of course you have to type it all out. Not much free time for you, is there, Cathy?'

'Enough, I'm enjoying it. Both the story and the work.'

'What about weekends. Like today, for instance. Surely she doesn't work then?'

'Sometimes. Depends how it's going.'

Grant looked thoughtful. 'I used to envy successful authors,' he said, 'but I don't know. It's a pretty lonely job by the sound of it. We could stay in with her this evening when we get back if you like.'

'Heavens, she isn't lonely. She has dozens of friends in Venice. What I mean is that when she stays in to work it is usually because she chooses to do so, not because she has nowhere to go.'

They finished their drink and their tour of Burano, then boarded the steamer to take them the short distance to Torcello. Grant was a good guide and Cathy told him so.

'Ah when I have an interesting and intelligent companion it is a pleasure. Cathy I have enjoyed today so much.' He put his arm round her, drawing her close to him, 'and it isn't over yet. The night is young Catherine – do they ever call you Catherine?'

'No, I've been Cathy ever since I can remember, but I was christened Catherine. Catherine Grace.'

'Pretty like you,' he murmured against her ear.

They went for a meal when they returned to Venice, and walked home beneath the stars, and for the first time for many weeks Cathy felt utterly content.

On Monday morning she received two letters, the first since arriving in Italy. One was from her mother, who she had spoken to on the telephone during the first week. It didn't say a lot, mostly that she was lucky to be in the sun as Britain was having a fairly wet spring. The other letter was from her friend Linda. It was a long, newsy letter, telling her the latest office gossip, for they had both worked for the same company, then going on to a list of discos and theatre going she had indulged in for the last few weeks. Page five started, 'a change of subject now, Cathy. I wasn't sure if I should mention this, but guess it's better for you to know now, and from me, as you and I talked about it a little. Steve is getting married in two weeks' time – they got a special licence. I know this is true because his new girlfriend is a friend of a friend of my brother. Of course your mother may have told you all this as Steve lives so near to your home, but I haven't seen your mum since you left, and I'm really keeping my promise to let you know how it goes with him if I can. Now I want a long letter from you, telling me how you are making out in Venice. At least you are missing this horrible weather we are having. I miss our chats, and am already looking forward to your return, so don't get turned on by any of those handsome, dark eyed Venetians, will you? Chow. (See, I know one Italian greeting!) Write soon, love from Linda.'

She was reading her letters in the bedroom, the post having arrived as she left the breakfast table. So, Steve hadn't wasted any time with his new love. It wasn't a nice feeling. She didn't think it was jealousy, well only a little, because she had come to terms with the knowledge that she hadn't loved him the way she should have done for a marriage. How many people did, she wondered now. And how many drifted into marriage because they were fond of each other, felt a certain physical attraction, and were ready to settle down. And so often it worked – unless they met someone and couldn't live without him. Well that was how she wanted it to be. She had been willing to accept less once, but not anymore. She smiled to herself over Linda's remark about the handsome, dark eyed Venetian. Grant was dark eyed, but there the description ended, for he was neither Italian, nor really handsome in a conventional sense. Yet he appealed to her. His earnest way of delving into every detail. 'A writers mind,' he said when she had laughed at the amount he wanted to know.

'I've always enjoyed research, liked finding out about everything. If I had been a woman I would have spent my time gossiping over the garden wall I shouldn't wonder.'

That was something else which attracted her, his sense of humour. They had arranged to meet again on Wednesday evening.

'How long will you be in Venice?' she asked.

'Hard to tell. I came to research this book and, well I'll tell you Cathy, but I've not mentioned it to anybody else, I have recently received a legacy from an uncles will, so I can afford to indulge my passion for wanting to write a book, for a while. What I mean is that I'm not tied for a few months. I couldn't spend more than a year here of course, although it was a substantial amount. I shall need to work again but, meanwhile I'm what you might possibly call "a gentleman of leisure" at present.'

Scott telephoned early Monday morning. 'Cathy, are you free this evening. I'd like to take you out.'

'No,' she said, 'I'm not.'

'If you are remembering our last encounter, I promise I will not talk about what you, I know, regard as nonsense. I am asking you out as one person to another, a male attracted to a female. I simply wish to buy you a meal and enjoy your company.'

'Scott you stagger me, you really do. After prowling around the bedroom as you did, on whatever pretext, do you really think I would consent to being seen in public with you?'

'Yes, I do. I explained what happened.'

'I never told my aunt that I disturbed you there, you know. I suppose because I half believed what you told me about an intruder. Yet the more I think about it the more I wonder if I have been taken for a ride.'

'No Cathy, you haven't. I fall short in both yours and my estimation over many things, but what I told you was the truth. Someone was in your aunt's bedroom that evening.'

They arranged an evening out on Tuesday, and as the time drew near she wondered what had made her succumb because so far they had quarrelled almost every time they were together. 'With my quick rising temper, which heaven knows I *do* try to control, and his obstinacy, we don't stand a chance' she said to her reflection in the mirror as she brushed her curly hair which had fallen into natural ringlets as it had grown to below shoulder length. She decided to have it cut as soon as possible. Mary was talking about a weekend soon on Lake Garda where she had friends.

'They have a lovely villa, large grounds, a swimming pool, and they are dear people. You are invited too, in fact they want to meet you very much.'

I'll have my hair cut before we go, she promised herself. Better for swimming, and a lot easier for me to manage.

Mary was well into her stride with the new book and Cathy became immersed in the story during the daytime working hours. She typed the day's dictation each evening when they finished, and gave the weeks work to Mary every Friday night.

Her evening with Scott began very low-key. Ginette answered the doorbell and brought him upstairs where Mary promptly offered him a drink. 'Or are you both in a hurry?' she asked. Scott didn't consult her, as she was sure Grant would have done.

'Not at all,' he said, sitting down opposite Mary and stretching his long legs out.

'You know I envy you, Mrs Fielding, being able to spend six months here and six back home. Only if it were me I might be tempted to turn it around and have the winter out here...'

Mary dimpled up at him. 'Winter here isn't all that special, and most of my friends are here during the summer. How is your convalescence? Betty told me you were recovering from an injury.'

Cathy couldn't decide if he was trying to annoy her by his seeming indifferent, if he was being extra polite to Aunt Mary, or merely being his usual egocentric self. She tossed the last of her drink down so quickly that it almost choked her, and she seethed inwardly when she saw he had noticed and his eyes were laughing at her.

If he goads me into losing my temper he'll regret it, she vowed silently. The arrogant, self-opinionated prig. I've a good mind to call off our date... Yet she knew she wouldn't as he rose to his feet, genially thanking Mary for her hospitality, then bestowing a dazzling smile on Cathy herself. Dammit, against my will almost, he seems to hypnotise me, she thought.

Once outside he touched her arm gently, but in a proprietary fashion. 'You look stunning tonight,' he said simply, 'you are a very beautiful woman, Cathy.'

She kept silent because he sounded as though he meant it and she wanted to believe him. She couldn't prevent excitement rising in her. However much she detested his attitudes and mannerisms, he attracted her in a way no other man had previously been able to.

They ate in a trattoria in a small square not far from St. Marks. 'Betty and Guy especially recommended this one,' he told her.

It looked welcoming, with red and white check cloths, candles in bottles, and small bouquets of real flowers in unglazed pottery vases on the tables. The menu was expansive, and she chose pasta, followed by fish, and Italian ice-cream as a dessert. They drank a sweet white wine and they talked. At first about paintings, and as the evening wore on about their lives up to the present time. Afterwards they walked to St.Mark's and joined the throng of people who were soaking up the atmosphere of the square. They window shopped, admiring much of the Venetian glass on display and abhorring some of the other.

'Made for the tourist trade,' Scott said, laughing with her at one particularly ugly specimen in the front of a window.

'Yet it might make someone very, very happy,' she countered, 'a reminder of the holiday of a lifetime. I can imagine that piece, which I personally find repulsive, looking right on a mantelpiece in someone's home.'

'Yes, so can I, Cathy.' His hand reached for hers, 'It's easy for us to laugh because we cannot see beauty in that, but most things are beautiful for someone. Come on, shall we have a drink?'

It was the first time he had actually consulted her about anything, and she was so amazed that she didn't answer.

'Or aren't you ready for one yet?' he said quickly.

'Yes, I'd love one.'

'Right, which place takes your fancy?'

'What here? In the square?'

'Why not? Everyone ought to dine or drink in San Marco at least once while they are here.'

They selected a café with tables under the columns, and while they were waiting for their order to arrive she looked about at the souvenir sellers with their yo-yos and snowstorms of Venice, their balloons, windmills and novelties, and turning toward her companion she said softly, 'You know, this time a month ago I didn't dream I would be experiencing anything like this. Scott, life can be very, very exciting sometimes.'

His hand touched hers briefly across the width of the table, 'And never more so than at this moment,' he said.

It was late when Cathy climbed into her bed that night, and the memory of Scott's goodnight kiss stayed with her until morning. She could not hate a man who made her feel so excited, she couldn't believe he was not what he pretended to be.

During the evening he never once mentioned the proposed robbery of her aunt's jewels which had haunted their previous meetings. For the first time since she had set eyes on him Scott behaved like a normal male in the presence of a normal female. Cathy responded with the softer side of her nature, which she sometimes suspected only she knew about.

She fell asleep quickly, although she planned to stay awake for a while to relive the amazing contentment and inevitability she felt at the uniting of two minds and hearts that had taken place this evening. The harsh sound of her alarm clock woke her the next morning in less benevolent state of mind. Even the thought of an evening with Grant failed to disperse her black mood. Halfway through the morning dictation Mary broke off to ask her if she was all right.

'Yes.' Even to herself her voice sounded bad tempered as she snapped out the single word. At eleven thirty Mary stopped again. 'I think we'll pack it in for this morning, Cathy,' she said quite mildly. 'If you still insist you are feeling quite well then I suggest you go for a walk and try to clear the gloom from your mind, because it's overshadowing our work.'

Cathy flushed guiltily as she closed her notebook.

'Back at two please.' Mary's voice was quiet, and her blue eyes held a serious expression that Cathy felt boded ill for her should she lose her temper without good reason.

'I'll be here,' she said, and hurried out. In the security of her room she flung herself onto the bed and punched her fists into the pillow, weeping with anger and frustration without knowing why. Later she did go out and walk, but the little alleys and squares were not conducive to letting off steam the way a brisk walk along a seaside promenade or through a park or long, long road back home in England, was.

As the sun reached its fiercest she returned, and finding no-one about in the kitchen, took a long cold orange drink upstairs and sat on her balcony watching the movement of water and traffic far below. She consciously tried to relax and ask herself why she felt she would like to bang everyone's heads together today. As she grew calmer the only reason she could offer was the worry of the knowledge she possessed about her aunt's jewel collection, and the frustration of not knowing how involved Scott Underwood was.

Forty eight hours ago I was only concerned that he wanted it kept secret from Mary, only bothered in case someone *was* planning to rob her, she thought, but since last night… her eyes filled with angry tears. I wish I had never set eyes on him, wish we had never kissed.

She was downstairs with her pad and pencil, a clean cool frock on, by five minutes to two. She had brushed her chestnut hair until it shone, and tied it back from her face with a bright pink bow, and she smiled at Mary when she entered the room a few moments afterwards. To Cathy's relief her aunt didn't cross question her, she simply smiled back and said, 'Hullo, all set to go? I've had a bit of a rethink over what we did this morning. This is the beginning of the chapter again. Leave the other and I'll look at both versions when you've typed them out.'

They worked until nearly five o clock then Mary said, 'Enough I think. Let's call it a day. Like a drink?'

They sat on the balcony in companionable silence for a while, then Cathy leapt up, 'I forgot to tell Ginette I'll be out for dinner tonight,' she said.

'Goodness, girl, you startled the living daylights out of me.' Cathy made her apologies to Ginette. 'It is all right, signorina. I have cold meal tonight, very simple salad.'

Cathy returned to the balcony. 'I'm dining with Grant this evening,' she told Mary.

'Ah. He is very good looking, and seems able to converse about many subjects, yet he still puzzles me slightly.'

Feeling more her old self after the orderly stint of work this afternoon, Cathy said, 'What puzzles you about him?'

'Where his money comes from? What his background is? And what his motives are? Sorry, take no notice of me, Cathy – it is a very bad habit of mine to always try to work out these things about people. It's the frustrated crime writer in me I suspect. The romantic who longs to be the detective.'

'I can enlighten you about some of your queries,' Cathy said. 'Grant was left some money recently in his uncles will. He told me so the other evening. Enough he said, to enable him to come out here for a while to write a book. I told you he was writing a book, didn't I?'

'Yes dear, you did. Oh well, nothing very sinister then. Has he relatives out here, or friends?'

'The friend where he is staying I believe. I don't know where it is. Think I'll get myself prettied up now.' She turned before she reached the door, 'I'm – sorry about this morning, Mary. I don't often have such black moods, and I shouldn't have let it show.'

'Forget it. I have. Probably a bit of homesickness. But if anything does trouble you, Cathy, about the work or outside problems, I'm a good listener, my dear. Don't bottle it up and keep it to yourself, will you? Off you go then and have a pleasant evening.'

CHAPTER 6

Grant was more boisterous than she had known him when they met that evening. 'Let's walk for a while first,' he said, 'work up an appetite.'

Cathy glanced down at her shoes, and he said, 'Maybe you'd rather not. OK we'll go straight to a restaurant.'

'No,' she said quickly, 'these are comfortable if a bit flimsy, and as long as we aren't doing a five mile hike I shall be all right.'

'Sure?'

She smiled at him. 'Quite sure, Grant.' He put his arm round her shoulder as they crossed the square and both of them would have been very surprised if they had looked back and upwards at that moment, for standing by the window in the spare bedroom and watching them, was Mary.

They walked a long way, but Cathy couldn't be sure when they finally entered a restaurant that it was, after all, so far from their starting point. Grant knew Venice as she did not, but from her own wanderings she realised you could weave in and out among the alleys and squares, simply going round in circles. Yet why should Grant do that – he knew his way about. Mary's searching mind would find a reason she was sure, and she smiled to herself as she reflected that working with her aunt she was beginning to absorb some of her ways.

'What are you smiling about?' Grant asked, pleasantly enough.

'Oh I was thinking about my aunt's analytical mind,' she said. 'She would love to write detective stories you know, but because her romances do so well she keeps the unravelling of mysteries to her private life.'

'I didn't know that.'

She looked at him and wondered at the sharpness in his tone. 'No reason why you should of course. Maybe we always want something that is not for us. The grass is always greener, you know.'

'Maybe. How is her book going anyway?'

'Quite well. And yours?'

They were sitting inside the café now, and with the fork halfway to his mouth he paused, 'This may surprise you but I've written two chapters,' he said.

'I'm glad. I wish it luck, Grant.'

It was a delicious meal, but there was an atmosphere that she hadn't encountered before in her outings with him. She couldn't quite put her finger on it, but there was definitely something wrong. Grant seemed as suave, as composed, as attentive as ever, and yet it seemed to her that it was an act, and half of him wasn't taking part at all. Mentally she shook herself. This was ridiculous, it must be a legacy from her black mood of yesterday and she must snap out of it. They finished their meal and Grant reached into his back pocket for his wallet. She was draping a silk shawl around her shoulders when she realised something was wrong.

'What is it, Grant. What's the matter?' she asked.

Frantically patting and searching his trouser pockets he said dramatically, 'I've been robbed. My wallet's gone.'

They searched the immediate area after she had paid for the meal. 'What a blessing you brought some money with you,' Grant said. 'I'll pay you back of course.'

'Nonsense, it's about time I paid for a meal. Hadn't we better report your loss to - to someone. The police?'

'Yes, yes, the polizia, but first let's retrace our steps in case it simply fell out.'

When she hesitated, wanting to report the theft first, he pulled her along roughly, 'All in good time, Cathy. I'll look silly if I report it and then find it on the way back.' So they retraced their steps, and as they had walked such a long way to begin with Cathy knew they would never find the wallet.

'Even if you dropped it, or pulled it out accidently, someone will have picked it up by now,' she argued.

They finally emerged into the little square behind Mary's house. 'Would you like to 'phone from Aunt Mary's?' she said.

'Thank you.'

Mary was sitting on the balcony watching the movements on the canal below. She turned as they entered the room.

'Hullo, my dears. It's so cool and lovely here this time of the evening. Come and sit down. Would you like a drink? There's sherry, gin, sangria or fruit juice.'

'Not for a moment,' Cathy said quickly, 'but may Grant use the telephone, his wallet has been stolen?'

Mary's eyes sparkled. 'Really. Phone in the hall Grant. I'll pour you both a drink while you report it, then come back and tell me what happened. You're both all right, you weren't hurt, were you?' She added, suddenly alarmed.

'No. Didn't even see it happen,' Cathy assured her, while Grant went into the hall to telephone.

'I'll just change my shoes,' Cathy said, pulling a wry face, 'do you know we walked miles tonight. In this city of gondolas, vaporetti and water-taxis, we walked! Maybe it wasn't so far, but it seemed like miles and miles to me in these shoes.'

Grant was by the telephone as she went by. 'Thank you. Grazie,' she heard him say. When she came downstairs he was talking to Mary.

'What are they going to do?' Cathy asked.

'Not much they can do at present. I've given them details, now I shall have to wait and see what turns up.'

'But didn't they want to see you. Talk to you face to face?'

He swung round to look at her properly. 'Good heavens, whatever for? I told them what had happened. That it was in my pocket when I left home but not when I went to pay the bill. Presumably they will check the café staff too, but...' he shrugged, 'I doubt if I'll ever see wallet or money again.'

'I doubt it too,' Mary said, 'was there much money in it, Grant?'

'Several million lire. Cards, personal documents.'

'I can lend you some money to tide you over,' Mary said suddenly. And going towards the armchair the other side of the room she picked up her handbag which was beside it and took out her cheque book.

'No, please. It is most kind of you Mrs Fielding, but I couldn't possibly accept. I can sort it out with my bank.'

He stayed for another hour and took the notes Mary held out to him before he left. 'In case you need money before the bank opens tomorrow,' she said, smiling at him, 'and these are a gift, not a loan.'

Cathy went downstairs to see him out and he took her in his arms and kissed her hard and almost viciously, leaving her breathless and slightly bruised.

'I'm sorry about this evening.' His voice was steely, 'I feel pretty grim about it.'

'It wasn't your fault, Grant.'

'I'll be in touch,' he said, and walked briskly away without looking round. Cathy sighed and went back upstairs in a thoughtful mood.

'That was a bad do,' Mary said when she joined her again.

'Yes. Grant was in an odd mood all evening though, even before that happened.'

'Was he?'

'I thought so. Unless it's me. I've been in a strange mood too this last couple of days, haven't I?'

'Maybe we need a break dear. You know I mentioned going to see friends in Garda for a few days? Let's make it soon, shall we? Not next week because I'm committed on several evenings, and Betty and Guy will be here this coming Sunday for lunch. How are you fixed for about ten days' time? Its Wednesday now, say Friday week and we could stay until the Monday to make a nice long weekend. What are your plans for that far ahead?'

Cathy laughed delightedly. 'Nil,' she said, 'and I'd love to see Garda. The pictures you've sent me of it in the past are enchanting; but will your friends really want me too because it's all right you know Mary, I can amuse myself here. I mean, well I don't want to push in,' she finished weakly.

'You won't be. They especially asked me to bring you because I've talked to them about you so much. Right, that's settled then, because all they are waiting for from me is a date. I hope Grant finds his wallet. It is just possible, isn't it, that he could have left it at home? Tom was always leaving things he needed in his other trousers when he changed to go out I remember.'

Cathy shook her head. 'He would have known,' she said.

Grant did not telephone the following day, nor yet on Friday, and when they finished work for the weekend Cathy said to her aunt, 'I hope Grant is making out all right Mary. I've not heard nor seen him since Wednesday evening when his money was stolen.'

'Do you know where he is living?' Cathy shook her head again.

'No. Only that he is staying with a friend, or in a friend's apartment. I've no idea what part of Venice, or even his friend's name.'

'Do you know if he is English or Italian, this friend? Because the English living here are much easier to trace.'

Cathy shook her head again. 'Not even that. It hasn't seemed important until now.'

She had not yet typed Wednesday and Thursdays dictation, so with today's it meant three sessions to catch up and Friday evening looked like being a busy one. At half past nine Mary came and tapped on her door.

'Come in.' Cathy swivelled round from the desk where she was typing.

'Do you feel like coming for a drink, love? Betty just phoned, and I'm meeting them in Harry's Bar. Scott is coming too.'

Cathy looked at the work. 'Well this is the last sheet. Yes, I'd like to, thanks. Can you give me ten minutes to sort this out and get ready?'

'Of course.'

They all met outside Harry's Bar.

'It's pretty crowded,' Guy said, 'I've just looked in, but maybe a drink and a quick mingling. You always see so many people you know in there, then we could all go somewhere quieter. What do you think?'

In the general agreement that followed Scott murmured in her ear, 'I'm so glad you came.' Then they were all being jostled as they almost fought their way into the interior of Harry's Bar. Conversation was impossible, and when somebody tried to walk past her with a tray of drinks, it jolted her even closer to Scott, who promptly put his arm round her waist and grinned like a schoolboy at her. It was far too noisy to attempt even a silly joke about it so she simply grinned back and thought to herself what a difference in this man since their first meeting. Almost as though he trusted her now, when he hadn't done so before, although that seemed ridiculous because he hadn't known her before. It was while these ideas were running round in her excited head that she saw Grant. He was sitting in a corner with another man and they were deep in conversation. If he had looked up he would have seen her, but he never raised his head, and seconds later the gap between them was filled with yet another body fighting his way either to or from the bar, and Scott was saying, 'Surely that is Grant Taggart over there.'

For a moment she was tempted to pretend she hadn't seen him, but she had never been good at telling even the smallest white lie and in any case what reason did she have for not recognising him.

'Yes, but how did you know his name Scott? He didn't know you.'

'You've discussed this.' His voice was hard as steel and his brown eyes glittered dangerously.

'What do you mean, discussed it? You turn every conversation into an interrogation Scott. Of course we didn't discuss you, but as you seemed to know him before meeting him at Mary's party, I, foolishly perhaps, imagined you had met somewhere. I was wrong, and Grant assured me he did not know you.'

'Be careful what you tell him Cathy. I can't get a line on him...'

'Oh, you're insufferable –' she stepped away and the man she bumped into spilt his drink, splashing it over his companion's dress, and in the general confusion of apologies Cathy felt herself being observed. Moving her head very slightly she saw Grant watching her. He smiled, inclined his head, then moved out of her vision through the crowded bar.

They left soon afterwards and went to a small restaurant. Cathy still felt angry, but Scott chatted and laughed his way through the next hour without mentioning Grant Taggart again. Walking back across St. Mark's Square he contrived to let other people separate the two of them from Mary, Betty and Guy.

'Why must you always be so touchy?' he said, 'I'm not being jealous or spiteful, or unfriendly, or any of the labels you may think of when I warn you about talking too much to the wrong people, Cathy. I am as sure as I can be that a plan is afoot to steal your aunt's jewel collection.'

'And you think Grant is involved in this – this plan?' Her voice rose scornfully.

'I never said that. I only said I know nothing about him. Nobody seems to.'

'You mean you've – you've actually been snooping around trying to find out about him. Do you do that with everyone you don't know about? Did you cross question your aunt and uncle about me that first night we met. Did you check-'

He took hold of her arm. 'Steady on, Cathy. I'm warning you for your own good. Grant Taggart may be a perfectly genuine chap, but someone is masterminding this gang, and so far we haven't a suspicion who he is, so of course I check everything and everybody, especially –'

Angrily she pulled her arm away. 'Well I think you're dreaming the whole thing. It's a figment of your imagination. If it isn't then tell my aunt. Warn her. If not then stop testing out your stupid theories on me Scott Underwood, because it won't wash. I simply do not believe them.'

'Keep your voice down –'

'I won't, any more than I'll listen to your nasty thoughts about my friends. It's contemptible the way you carry on.'

Mary, Betty, and Guy were standing still to allow them to catch up and they all walked back to the flat together.

'See you on Sunday,' Mary said as they waved goodnight.

'You all right, Cathy, you look a bit flushed,' she said when they were upstairs.

'Yes thanks.'

'It's great isn't it, Betty and Guy have been invited to Garda the same weekend as us,' her aunt's voice went on, and Cathy turned quickly to look at her.

'Just – just Betty and Guy?' she said, aware of the two spots of temper still glowing on her cheeks.

'I believe Scott is included, but isn't certain of his movements yet. I hope he comes Cathy, it will be younger company for you. Well I'm for bed now. Goodnight dear, sleep well.'

'Goodnight.' Cathy said faintly, wondering now how she could avoid going to Garda with Mary next weekend.

Sleep eluded her for hours as she relived the evening. The thrill, and in the privacy of her bed she admitted to herself she had felt a thrill when Scott's arm came round her in the bar. Then the revulsion, the anger she felt with him. He was like two people, the one arrogant and bossy, the other compassionate and gentle, and there seemed no bridge between them. Which was the real Scott, she wondered. Which was the man beneath the policeman? Was he always suspicious, always dictatorial? Yet the evening she spent with him so recently when they discovered how perfectly in tune they could be had been magical. She found herself remembering every expression, every inflection in Scott's voice, and pulling the cotton sheet up to her shoulders she closed her eyes and tried not to think further about him. With luck he wouldn't be at Garda when she and Mary were there. Surely when he knew that she would be a guest he would plead other business, for she thought he could no more want to spend the weekend being thrown together as they would be, than she did. Angrily she brushed away the tear that escaped from her tightly closed eyes. 'I won't let you rile me Scott Underwood, either with your foolish notions or your highhanded manner,' she murmured chokily, then quickly turning onto her stomach she buried her face in the pillow and tried to shut out the image of his golden hair and deep seeing brown eyes.

CHAPTER 7

Grant telephoned the Wednesday before they were going to Garda.

'Sorry I haven't been in touch Cathy,' he said cheerily, 'I had business away from Venice, but I'm back now and longing to see you. Can you make it tonight?'

She had planned an evening of chores, washing her hair, writing letters, mending.

'Yes, of course. How are you?'

'On top of the world. And you?'

'I'm fine,' she answered cautiously. 'I have wondered how you were though. I mean with having your wallet stolen. Did you recover it Grant?'

'No. Still, can't cry over spilt milk. It's one of those things that happen. I'll pick you up around eight this evening. OK?'

'Fine,' she said.

She told Ginette she would be out for dinner. 'Sorry it's such short notice. Grant only telephoned lunchtime.'

Ginette smiled at her, 'Not to worry,' she said in her careful English, 'you are young, beautiful, and in Venice.'

Cathy hugged her. 'I know what you mean,' she said, 'somehow, even if you don't intend it to, the romance gets you.'

'Gets you?' Ginette looked puzzled, but Cathy hugged her again and laughed softly, 'You live in a magical city, Ginette.'

She wore a multi-coloured dress and a plain black shawl for her date with Grant.

'Cathy, you are lovely,' he said. They ate at a café near the Rialto, and Grant seemed not to have a care in the world. He dismissed her concern for him lightly. 'I meant to let you know, but I'm a poor correspondent Cathy. And I wasn't certain how long I should be gone. I knew you weren't lonely of course – I saw you with superman in Harry's Bar on Friday soon after I got back.'

She found herself sticking up for Scott. 'Don't say that in such a derogatory way,' she said, but he only laughed.

'He's too good to be true, Cathy. No-one could have such looks and be genuine.'

'Oh Scott's genuine,' she said quickly, surprised at herself. Grant pulled a face, 'OK, if you say so, but I can't imagine what we are thinking about to talk of someone else when we are together. Cathy I've missed you, do you realise that? Let's make up for it now and at the weekend. We shall both have two completely free days then, so where would you like to go?'

'Sorry, I shall be away at the weekend.'

'Away. Where?'

'We're going to Garda, to some friends of my aunts.'

He scowled at her across the red and white checked tablecloth.

'Do you have to go?'

'Don't *have* to, it's not part of the job of course, but I'd like to. Anyway I've already agreed and to tell the truth I am looking forward to seeing one of the lakes.'

'Ah well, it can't be helped I suppose. What place are you favouring with your presence?'

'Sarcasm doesn't suit you Grant, but we're going to Gargnano.'

He didn't mention the weekend again and when, a little later in the evening as they were strolling back by the Grand Canal she asked which city he had been in for the past week he wouldn't tell her. He didn't refuse point blank. 'Several actually,' he said, 'dodging about you know, here and there.' Then he swiftly changed the subject.

Perhaps Grant is a married man she thought later, when she was back home. He was certainly evasive about where he had been since the night his wallet was stolen.

'I'll telephone you on Monday after your return from Garda,' he said when he kissed her goodnight, then added, almost grudgingly, 'I hope the sun shines on Garda for you.'

Maybe it was simply pique because now he was back in Venice he had plans for them both for the weekend, but it looked suspiciously as though he was already taking her for granted. She thought it was a good thing she would not be available this weekend after all, for although she admitted to herself that he most definitely attracted her, it was too soon after Steve to think in those terms about anyone else. It was balm to her wounded pride though that he seemed to enjoy her company as much as she did his, but it puzzled her that he was so reticent about his movements over the last week. For someone who admits he is curious about other people and expects them to be so about him, it was strange. Briefly she thought of mentioning it to Mary. Her puzzle solving mind would undoubtedly weave some kind of explanation, but would it be near the truth or would it be a figment of her imagination? Anyway, she told herself, he couldn't have missed me all that much in spite of what he said, because he's been home since last Friday, and so that's one weekend he missed out for a start.

Thursday and Friday were spent tying up the loose ends of the chapter Mary had been working on all week. She wasn't happy with the middle of it, and one alteration led to another, and soon the chapter was scrapped and rewritten from a new angle. It was almost six o clock on Friday evening when they finished.

'Thanks, Cathy. I know I get carried away sometimes, but I did want to get it right before we left. Now I can relax and enjoy the weekend.'

They planned to make an early start on Saturday morning. Betty and Guy were taking their car and they would all travel together. To Cathy's relief Scott was not to be one of the party. When Mary had mentioned this a few days previously Cathy was surprised at the disappointment which surged through her body, then she realised it wasn't disappointment at all but relief. Now she wouldn't have to keep such a curb on her temper, which she knew flared fiercely too often.

'Will you ever learn to stop and think before you speak, Cathy?' her mother used to warn her, and she usually regretted the things she did and said in the rush of immediate reaction.

She managed to fit in a visit to the hairdresser Thursday lunchtime and while she was packing Friday evening Mary popped into her room. 'Take a swimsuit,' she advised, 'Jean and Ian have a super pool.' She was in bed by ten thirty, after setting her alarm for six the next morning. Betty and Guy were calling for them at eight. 'We'll travel before it gets too hot,' Mary said, 'and we need not leave for our return until sometime on Monday.'

They were waiting in the hall when Guy came in for them. 'Good morning girls, all set?' He sounded fresh and cheerful and beamed at them both as he picked up the two small weekend cases and led the way outside. They walked to the Piazzale Roma and approached the dark green Mercedes. As they drew near Cathy saw there were already two people in the car. Betty sitting in the back, and in the driver's seat, and grinning at her as she approached, was Scott Underwood.

'You get in the front Cathy,' Guy said, 'and us old fogies will reminisce together.' He stowed the cases in the boot and the three of them settled themselves as she silently climbed into the seat next to Scott.

'This is an unexpected pleasure,' he said in his normal voice, adding in a whisper, 'but not for you judging by the expression on your face at this moment.' He turned his head slightly, 'All comfortable back there? Right, Gargnano here we come.'

As the car moved smoothly away he said very quietly and without looking at her, 'You're scowling.'

Cathy's feelings were in a turmoil. Remembering their last stormy meeting she was amazed he seemed so friendly. Of course he was behaving this way purposely to annoy her. In the short time they had known each other he did so with unerring instinct. Well this time would be different. This time she would show him she didn't care how dictatorial he was for she would take no notice whatsoever. She would smile with icy and distant politeness, she would incline her head in regal fashion as though whatever he mentioned was too stupid for her to bother with. That had been half the trouble, she reflected silently now, the fact that she jumped each time he set a trap...

'I hope Mary brought everything she needs,' he said, breaking into her thoughts. 'You will of course, know the items I'm specifically referring to.'

'It's nothing to do with you so kindly keep your nose out of our affairs,' she snapped, knowing her face was flushed with anger which she tried hard to suppress at that moment because of the three people sitting and talking so happily in the back of the car.

He chuckled wickedly. 'It's so easy to make you mad, Cathy. Do you realise that?'

'If you weren't driving you would see and *feel* how mad I am,' she said through tight lips. 'I'm trying to keep it in right now out of consideration for the rest of the company, but if you push me too far I won't be answerable for the consequences. I don't much care if it spoils your weekend, but I do care that the others enjoy themselves.'

He was silent for a few moments and she gazed unseeingly out of the window. Then he spoke quietly, 'All right, Cathy. A truce for the weekend, because it's almost certain we shall be thrown together quite a lot, being the youngsters of the party so to speak. Tell me what you've been doing with yourself since last Friday?'

Cathy took a deep breath and decided quickly that this was the only way the weekend would be bearable, and embarked on a light hearted recital of their week, only omitting her date with Grant on Wednesday. It was reasonably easy to keep the conversation friendly after that because they were both trying, and as the scenery grew more beautiful Cathy felt herself truly relaxing.

Jean and Ian were welcoming, and as she changed into a bikini in her room, which overlooked Lake Garda itself, she felt a thrill of pleasure run through her body at the prospect of the hours ahead. The villa seemed to have been built halfway up a mountain, and when she stepped outside onto the balcony, far below her was the shimmering water of Garda, while above were olive trees, and as her gaze went higher still, the crags, hollows and grandeur of the mountain out of which the villa had sprung.

The Italians were great artists, she thought, as she drank in so much beauty. Not only with paintings, for what other race could build modern villas into the scenery and make it look as if they had simply grown there.

She stepped back inside the room and closed the windows, then, slipping into the pink towelling robe she found hanging behind the bedroom door, she went downstairs. Jean had suggested drinks and lunch round the pool. 'We have a little summer house which protects us, and of course a few of those thatched umbrellas if you do wish to stay right beside the pool,' she told Cathy as she led the way out of the house. Scott was already there, looking marvellous in deep green satin trunks which enhanced the brown fitness of his body. She noticed the fine golden hairs on his legs and arms as he stood up to greet them, and she wished fervently at that moment that her own body could have been as tanned and glistening as his. Her arms and legs below the knees had caught the sun, and the V of her neckline too, where her dresses and tee shirts reached, but she was aware how white her shoulders and thighs must seem in comparison. Although most of May had been sunny she hadn't been to beaches or swimming pools to catch it even in her off duty hours.

Ian was a retired police inspector. Could that be what changed Scott's mind about coming, she thought, and was dimly surprised at the disappointment which surged through her body. Had she, deep down, hoped that it was because of her after all? She smiled her thanks as Ian led her to a white, ornately carved chair by an equally decorative table. 'Now a drink. What will you have?'

It was pleasant sitting there in the cool of the summerhouse, a warm swimming pool a matter of feet away, and she thought again how lucky she was to be here and wondered in a kind of daze what everyone she knew was doing in England now. Her mother, her friend Linda, Steve… Steve, was he married yet? When was it she had received Linda's letter? In a sudden panic she realised she couldn't remember what he looked like now, and the more she tried to visualise his features the harder it became. Even his voice was gone from her memory, yet she had practically grown up with Steve, had once been engaged to him – how could it all disappear so drastically?

The only voice and picture she had now was of a tall, bronzed male who looked something like she imagined the Greek Gods did, and the only voice in her heart seemed to be his deep and sometimes cynical one. For a second or two another picture flared in her mind's eye. A vision of a man with dark hair and inky eyes which mesmerised her, and of a voice that…

It was a woman's voice however that broke into her reverie. 'Cathy,' Mary was saying with a hint of amusement, 'you surely can't be dreaming of faraway sunlit places in this setting. Isn't it all so very beautiful?'

'Yes, and I'm still pinching myself to see if it is all true. Venice, and now this.'

She went for a swim before lunch. 'Safer,' Mary said, 'you need to wait an hour or so afterwards.' Scott joined her after a few moments, his length taking him easily through the water ahead of her.

'This is the life,' he said, as she caught him up at the far end of the pool, out of earshot of the rest of the party, 'swimming pool, sunshine, beautiful scenery and a beautiful companion – in reverse order.' His eyes were smiling as well as his lips. 'Race you back Cathy, come on.' He kept level with her for three quarters of the way, then shot ahead suddenly and was waiting as she reached the end.

'Beast,' she murmured, laughing at him.

'You look gorgeous,' he said, taking her hand, 'All shiny wet and glowing. Come on, luncheon is served I believe.'

They had fish for lunch, lemon sole served with a light, tingling white wine. Scott, who was sitting between Mary and Jean and opposite to Cathy, raised his glass silently in her direction, and a faint smile curved his lips and was echoed in his deep brown eyes. The gesture did not go unnoticed by Guy who was sitting next to Cathy.

'Scott's arm seems completely healed now,' he remarked quietly to her, 'when he first came out he couldn't raise it at all.'

After lunch they dispersed for siesta. 'Do please use the pool whenever you wish,' Jean said to Cathy and Scott. 'By about four o clock it will be a lot cooler,' she added.

Time went far too quickly. She wandered down to the village at four and Scott caught up with her halfway down the steep drive.

'Saw you from the balcony. Do you mind if I join you, Cathy?'

They bought postcards and stamps in the souvenir shop, wandered by the lake and watched the steamer making its graceful way through the water, then sat for a while outside a café with a long cool drink.

'I should like to paint this,' Scott said.

'Can you paint? I mean, I should like to as well but I'm no artist and it's the sort of remark – oh hell, I'm putting my foot in it again, aren't I? Only this time I really don't mean to,' she finished, mad with herself now for spoiling what could have been a pleasant afternoon. But Scott laughed. 'As a matter of fact I can. Not terribly well, but I think, and certainly hope that I improve a little each time. I've only tried portraits a couple of times, but I should very much like to paint you Cathy.'

She sat absolutely still and looked at him. Then, because he seemed so serious she answered quietly, 'Would you. Really?' He nodded.

'Why, Scott?'

'Why?' His voice too seemed quieter than usual.

'There's nothing much in me to paint. I mean I'm not the chocolate box type and I'm not wildly beautiful or cover girl looking...'

'Colours,' he said briefly, 'I should like to capture some of the glory on paper. That hair, it's like gleaming copper when the sun's on it, and your eyes, they're – *almost* green, and that lovely complexion,' he broke off as another couple sat down opposite them. They left then and walked back to Jean and Ian's where the rest of the party were back round the pool.

After dinner that evening they all went for a walk by the lake, and beneath a veranda of stars his hand found hers and it was as though a light had been switched on inside her. She felt the current race through her body and knew that this excitement had been underlying the antagonism this man evoked in her from the first moment they had met.

She meant to stay awake for a while after she was in bed, to relive that magical moment when she realised that she was in love with Scott Underwood, but she couldn't. The wine, the stars, and the heady knowledge that it was so combined to send her hurtling down the pathway of slumber and dreams. She awoke on Sunday morning feeling happier than she could ever recall before, and in those first few minutes of the new day, not quite realising why.

CHAPTER 8

They returned from Gargnano just after lunch on Monday. For the rest of that magical weekend Cathy realised now, she and Scott had not quarrelled again. Not only hadn't quarrelled, but had discovered each other's better qualities. Maybe we are all hiding our real selves, she thought, as a sort of protection. Whereas before she had seen Scott as brash and dictatorial, now she knew he was simply an efficient policeman and a man with a tidy mind and a vision. They went first to Guy and Betty's, then Guy loaded their luggage into his launch and took Mary and Cathy home. He left them on the landing stage.

'No point in tying up if you aren't coming in,' Mary said, smiling at him, 'see you again soon Guy.' How soon neither of them realised as they walked inside and entered the lift.

Ginette had been given several days off to visit her family. 'No need to rush back – Tuesday morning will do fine,' Mary told her, 'because I doubt if we shall return early on Monday and we can happily eat out in the evening and make our own breakfast Tuesday morning.'

Ginette's numerous relatives lived in and around Rome, and as two of her nieces were currently expecting a baby she was happy to be able to go on the trip.

Cathy was first out of the lift, and she turned and picked up Mary's case as well as her own. 'I'll carry them,' she said, preceding her aunt up the stairs to their bedrooms. As she negotiated the bend in the stairs she felt surprise that Mary's door was open, but it didn't prepare her for the chaos inside.

Drawers had been flung on the floor, their contents spewed across the room, the wardrobe cupboards had few clothes left on hangers, most were in a tumbled heap on the floor, as though someone had run through with a giant hand to pull them down. One or two were still crazily clinging lopsided to their padded hangers. The bedclothes had been tipped off and the mattress was askew on its base...

She heard the gasp behind her as Mary reached the door, and quickly she put the cases down and turned to put her arms round her. 'Whoever could have done such a thing?' Mary said, her voice full of tears, 'Oh Cathy, just look at it.'

She moved further into the room, shaking her nieces arm from her shoulders and bending down she picked up a blue chiffon scarf.

'Best to leave it I think,' Cathy said, 'fingerprints, you know.'

'Of course. I ought to have thought about that.' Mary dropped it forlornly and Cathy said gently, 'Shall I telephone the police, or Guy first?'

Guy and Betty both came along, and he took over from there, speaking rapidly in Italian to the police while Betty went into the kitchen to make some tea. It transpired that nothing had been taken. In answer to the question as to whether there was anything of value to take, Mary, now over her initial shock and more composed, said quietly, 'I have one or two nice pieces of jewellery, but as I was away for the weekend I was wearing them.'

The formalities over the police departed, and Betty and Cathy volunteered to clear up the mess, but Mary refused to leave them to it and sit downstairs with Guy.

'Three of us will have it finished faster than two,' she said, 'and I'm OK now, really I am. It was simply such a shock coming home from a lovely weekend and finding the place like this.'

Nevertheless, in spite of her brave words Cathy could see how shaken she still was. She felt terrible herself at the thought that someone had been prowling about in here while they were away, rifling through their private possessions.

Less than an hour later they had the room back to normal, on the surface anyway, although as Mary, looking strangely pale and sad now, said tremblingly, 'It looks the same as ever now, but it feels different.'

Scott arrived as Guy poured them all a drink. 'I'm so sorry, Mary,' he said, 'what a blessing you took them with you.'

'Yes. I've always said, and it still goes, they are only baubles, simply the trimmings of life. They can be replaced, but...' she hesitated, then looking directly at Scott, went on, 'it's surprising how much they come to mean to you, through associations and memories.'

'Yes I can understand that.' Scott's voice was gentle, and Cathy looked across the room towards him, but his attention was all for Mary at that moment. He never ceased to surprise her, instead of the interrogation she had expected him to direct at her aunt he was displaying an understanding that made her want to cry with love for him. Smiling her thanks to Guy she took the proffered drink and went to sit by Scott and Mary.

'I will confess I *almost* didn't take them all,' Mary was saying, 'but Guy had such faith in your judgement Scott, that I was swayed. I'm so thankful now that I was.'

'Mary, do you mean that you took all your jewellery with you to Garda on, on Scott's say so?' Cathy asked incredulously.

'Yes.'

'You don't usually take it then?'

'No, only the bits I expect to wear.'

'So did you have some kind of knowledge that this was likely to happen, Scott?' Cathy said, trying to control her flushing cheeks.

'Not really.' His casualness was infuriating. 'Only the facts I've known for some while, that there is a gang operating who only need the opportunity.'

'Then why didn't you let her leave them here and keep watch on the place yourself? You'd have caught them red handed then,' she snapped.

Guy's pleasant voice interrupted her. 'Steady on Cathy. Scott was invited for the weekend too. The fact that he offered some very sensible advice saved a robbery from what I can see of it. Nasty though this is,' he added.

'I didn't know you had them with you,' Cathy said, turning to Mary.

'I didn't want to worry you. Actually, after I had decided to take Scott's advice,' she turned to smile at him, her eyes suddenly twinkling, 'proffered very subtly through Guy, I wrapped them up, put them in my case and forgot them.'

Cathy almost literally bit her tongue. She mustn't add to the distress of the evening for Mary. She moved after a few moments to sit next to Guy, and Mary and Scott went on chatting. Inwardly Cathy was seething, but she tried, for her aunt's sake, to behave rationally.

'When does Ginette return?' she heard Scott say, but Mary's reply was too low to catch. Then Scott's penetrating tones again, 'I wonder if she mentioned to anyone the flat would be empty.' Guy and Betty joined in again now, but Cathy stayed silent, still fighting her anger that Scott, in spite of his previous remarks about not telling Mary of the dangers he predicted, should nevertheless have done so secretly.

Soon afterwards Betty rose. 'We'll be getting back then.'

'I'll be along later, I'll walk,' Scott said, and as Mary went as far as the lift with them he put out a hand to Cathy to restrain her from following.

'I don't know why you're so cross Cathy. If she hadn't taken them with her they would have been stolen by now.'

'Well you might have told me. You were the one who wouldn't mention this, this proposed robbery to Mary when I asked you to earlier. You wouldn't warn her or let anyone else do so, now suddenly, in a very sneaky manner you do. Oh it was very clever to get Guy to persuade her – and underhand.'

'Stuff and nonsense. You're behaving like a spoilt child because you knew nothing of it, and that wasn't deliberate, although the fewer people who knew the better of course.'

'Why? Don't you trust *anybody,* Scott? Do you think I would have blabbed to the thieves, whoever they are? Do you believe...' As Mary came back into the room Scott rose, 'I think it will be best if I go too,' he said apologetically to her, 'but could I come round to talk to you sometime tomorrow?'

'Yes, of course, Scott.' When he had gone – his 'goodnight Cathy' ignored, Mary yawned. 'I think I'll get to bed Cathy. I feel just about done in.'

'I'll make you another drink and bring it in,' Cathy said, 'and I'm sorry about that – that little fracas just now, but sometimes Scott can be unbelievably obtuse, Mary. Not that that is any excuse for quarrelling and adding to the strain.' She made some milky coffee and when she took it in Mary was in bed.

'Thank you dear, and don't be too hard on Scott, he is only trying to help.'

Back in her own room Cathy undressed, washed and slipped between the cool sheets. Her anger had subsided, and left in its place a bitter feeling of unhappiness. It seemed that every time she and Scott discovered they could enjoy each other's company to the exclusion of everything else, something cropped up which set all the old antagonisms whirring again. As a sob escaped from her throat she pushed her head into the pillow so as not to disturb or worry her aunt. She slept at last, but half woke several times during the night. When the alarm rang at seven she could easily have turned over and stayed in bed. They had cornflakes, croissants and coffee for breakfast, and talked about the days planned work and not about the break-in, nor even about the weekend at Garda. After washing up Mary said, 'Right, see you at nine, Cathy. We have a busy morning ahead of us.' She looked rather wan, as though she hadn't slept well either, but she seemed determined to be cheerful and Cathy followed her lead.

They worked steadily for an hour and a half, then Ginette returned and they broke for coffee and listened to her excited tale of the baby who arrived early.

'My favourite niece, and I was there to help,' she enthused, 'so lucky, so wonderful that I had the little holiday just then.'

'Ginette,' Mary said, as they cleared the cups away, 'we too had some excitement over the weekend, but not pleasant excitement as yours was.' Ginette listened, wide-eyed, as Mary told her of the attempted burglary while they were away.

'Oh Signora, so sad for you. I should have been here to help.'

At lunchtime there were two telephone calls, one for Mary from the polizia. 'Nothing really, simply checking to say they are working on the case. Wanted to make sure nothing was missing after all, they said that often it isn't discovered at the time, not unless it's obvious, and to let them know if we suddenly miss something. You know I ought to be enjoying the tracking down of the intruders Cathy, and I'm not.'

'I know.'

'It's the thought they were here routing about amongst my things I find hard to bear.' She shivered. 'Still, mustn't dwell on that I suppose. Obviously they were looking for my jewels, but I thought it was well not to tell the police I did have a reasonable collection and had taken them all with me. Might look as if I suspected someone had their eye on them, and really I hadn't.'

'So what did decide you to take them all?'

'Guy said Scott was not given to being an alarmist unduly. That it was one thing to be casual about them and quite another to be realistic. Scott you know had more than a suspicion something would happen.'

'Then he should have done something about it. Warned the local police, stayed behind himself and watched the place. It's easy enough to be glib and say I told you so after the event.'

'They wouldn't have listened, Cathy. And he didn't *know* it was going to happen. He thought it might sometime. There's a great difference.'

The other telephone call was for Cathy from Grant. 'Have a nice weekend, and are you free this evening?' he wanted to know. She checked with Mary first, reluctant to leave her if she might want company, then arranged to meet him at seven thirty.

Grant was in an exuberant mood. 'It seems ages since I saw you,' he said, holding out his arms.

This time she had comfortable sandals on her feet, and when he asked if she wanted to walk first and eat later, she happily acquiesced.

'Tell me about Garda. What did you do?'

'Ate, drank, swam, walked, and generally absorbed the lovely air and enjoyed the beautiful scenery.'

'By yourself?'

She laughed. 'What an odd question, Grant. Of course not, there were others there, seven of us altogether.'

'You and your aunt, your hosts, that's four?'

'One day your enquiring mind will get you into trouble Grant,' she answered lightly, 'Betty, Guy and Scott Underwood were also there.'

'Ah, superman himself. How long is he staying in Venice?'

She shrugged, ignoring his sarcastic and patronising way of referring to Scott, and he squeezed her hand and said quietly, 'No jumping to his defence this time I see. Perhaps he wasn't such a good companion for the weekend. If so I'm glad Cathy,' he said quickly, 'I mean I don't want you to like him too much.'

'I don't want to become involved with anyone Grant. I have my reasons. Let's keep it that way please.'

'Sure. No strings, Cathy my love. Now, where shall we eat?'

Cathy did not mention the break-in to Grant. The opportunity to bring it naturally into the conversation arose only once, when he asked after Mary, and she let it go by. 'She's fine,' she said, 'working hard...'

It was a pleasant evening but she didn't enjoy it as she felt she ought to. Walking home part of her mind was back in Garda remembering a walk beneath the midnight stars with Scott. Even his name seemed to make her heart beat faster, but it was no use, she couldn't possibly love him because she didn't even like him. He was pompous, overbearing, and now, behind her back he had given advice to Mary which, when she had suggested it, he had ridiculed.

They reached the entrance to Casa Ristori, Mary's apartment, and Grant pulled her gently towards him.

'Why Cathy, you're crying. What is it sweetheart, what's wrong?'

'I'm not crying.' Furiously she blinked away the tell-tale wetness, 'Something blew in my eyes. It's all right now.'

Expertly he swung her into his arms, his hands roamed across her back, dug into her shoulders; he buried her lips in his face, and when he finally released her she opened her eyes and looked straight into Scott's golden brown ones, as he stood on the bottom step watching them. With a little cry she ran past him and up the stairs. She had reached the landing door when Scott caught up with her. Reaching out he took the key from her hand. 'Very pretty. And how much did you tell lover boy about what happened while we were away? Come to that how much did you tell him *before* we went away?' He was still holding her hand which had grasped the key, and she brought her free hand up and delivered him a stinging blow across his cheek. He flinched and as his pressure on her lessened she wriggled free, took back the key and quickly went indoors. She was too angry to cry, almost too angry to think, and pleading a very bad headache to her aunt she went on upstairs to her bedroom.

'Scott came to see you,' Mary said quietly as she followed her, 'I think he wanted to apologise.'

'I know, I saw him,' she said thickly, stumbling up the last few stairs.

CHAPTER 9

Cathy was up early the following morning. As she sat on the pink velvet covered stool by the dressing table to brush her hair she tried to think rationally about the situation. Often she found the rhythmic brushing of her hair helped to gather her thoughts and ideas into order, but not today.

'You look a right mess, my girl,' she said ruefully to her image through the glass, 'a right mess.'

She was glad she had a job to do, it would stop her from dwelling on last night's fiasco, because she knew that she mustn't let her mind wander when she was working. Mary was a perfectionist over her work, and she didn't want to let her down.

Why, of all the people in the world, was she so attracted to the one man who antagonised her almost every time they met? Mutual, because she knew she had the same effect on him. And Grant, where did he fit in? She was attracted to him, very much so, but Scott had her heart, and she knew now that in spite of the odd moment when they seemed to have a wonderful rapport, a kind of magic, that was all it was. It stopped when they became ordinary people again, but not for her, only for Scott.

Mary seemed to have recovered her equilibrium, and before they began work she talked a little of the break-in.

'It shattered me more than I realised it would, if you see what I mean Cathy. I thought I wanted to write crime stories. I do want to, but having it brought so close to home gave me another perspective, and for a while it threw me. I'm OK now though, and wondering who knew there was anything worth stealing here, *and* the best time to strike.'

They stopped work early. 'Thought we could go and collect your ring Cathy,' Mary suggested, 'they telephoned to say it was ready. Then maybe a spot of lunch out. Does that appeal?'

'Very much, but can the lunch be my treat please? I would really like that, Mary.'

'That is nice of you dear. All right. I'll be ready in ten minutes, I've one telephone call to make before we go.'

Thirty minutes later, with the emerald ring glowing on her finger, Cathy sat opposite her aunt in the air conditioned restaurant.

'Do you know we've been here nearly six weeks already,' Mary said, smiling at her across the table. 'Six months seems a long while when you are thinking about it, but I've always found it rushes by so fast that it seems more like six weeks come the end. Are you enjoying Venice, Cathy? Glad you came?'

'Yes to both questions. How could anyone not enjoy Venice? It's as wonderful as I dreamed it would be, and working with you Mary is very good. In fact I think I shall find it hard to fit into any other job afterwards. It's absorbing and interesting, and I don't know why I should have been so lucky, but I am very grateful.' She blew her aunt a kiss.

'It's nice for me too because you fit in so well. Pippa always loves our trips to Venice. It's the first one she's ever missed.'

They talked of Pippa and of the rest of the family back home in England, then Mary said firmly, 'Back to the drawing board. I'd like to get them into Italy before we pack up tonight.' She was referring to the people in her book, who, in the story, were motoring down through France and into Italy, but with various stops on the way.

As they turned into the little piazza they saw Scott over the other side. Someone behind them called out to the waiter at the café, and Scott turned round and saw them. He raised his hand and Mary waved back, but Cathy ignored him and turned into the entrance to the apartment. They went straight to work, breaking only for tea when Ginette brought it in around three forty five.

'Signor Taggart called,' she told Mary, 'and said he would telephone later.'

'Thank you Ginette.' Turning to Cathy she said, 'Well that visitor would have been for you I think.'

'Scusi, Signora, it was *you* Signor Taggart wished to see.'

They worked until five, and Cathy pulled up the blind in her room and opened the window onto the balcony. The heat of the afternoon sun was over and the air felt cool and balmy. The sort of evening to be with someone you loved. She learned her arms on the wall of the veranda and looked out at the vista below and around her. The sights and sounds, colour and clatter of Venice's High Street, the Grand Canal. Sometimes it still seemed impossible to her that she was here in this city she had so often longed to visit. She found it incredible too that her thoughts were on relationships. After Steve she really only wanted to get away, not to become involved with anyone, for a while at least. Yet here she was attracted to two men – suave, dark eyed Grant who was usually such fun to be with and who gave her a sense of luxury and elegance. And Scott, the antithesis of his rival, with his thick golden hair and vital brown eyes. Why did even the thought of him send her into such shivering fantasies? Was it that his provocation was so strong that it sparked an answering stimulation in her? She felt the prickles of excitement rising again, and with a sudden movement turned from the film like scenes below her window and entered the room just as a sharp knock on her door was followed by Mary almost falling over herself in her rush to get inside.

'Mary, what is it?' Cathy said, as her eyes quickly took in the rather wild unnatural flush on her aunt's face.

'We've had burglars again. My dressing table drawers are open, well two of them are, and someone has obviously been rifling through the top one.'

Together they hurried into Mary's room, and Cathy said, a trifle unsteadily, 'Has anything been taken?'

'I – I don't know. I haven't really looked yet. I came straight in to you when I saw the disturbance.'

'I'll make you a cup of tea, because whoever did this,' she nodded her head towards the open drawers, 'obviously came in while we were at lunch or while we were working, and isn't around now.'

Mary went to the wardrobe, and opening it she reached inside. 'Still there,' she said with relief as she felt the bulk of her jewellery box. She came over and sat on the bed, then looked hard at her niece. 'I think we would have heard someone overhead if they came while we were in the house. I believe it must have occurred while we were at lunch. I never came up here afterwards, I used the bathroom downstairs, and we went straight into the drawing room to work, didn't we?'

Cathy nodded her head in agreement. 'Ginette was here, wasn't she?'

'Mmm. Let's go make that cuppa and have a word with her.'

Ginette was shocked and upset when Mary asked her if she had heard any noises in the bedroom at lunchtime while they were out, and told her the reason.

'But Signora, scassinatore again?'

'Afraid so, Ginette. Nothing missing so far as I can tell quickly, but there is no doubt someone came in. How I wonder? Could someone have swung along from another balcony, my window was on the catch and the blind was down.'

'Was the blind disturbed?' Cathy asked.

'No, but then a clever intruder, or should I say a methodical one, would be sure to straighten it out once he, or she, was in the room, wouldn't they? And if whoever it was left by the proper entrance... Ginette, where in the house were you during the time Cathy and I were out at lunchtime. Can you remember, Cara?'

Cathy walked over to the sink and filled the kettle while Ginette, looking flustered and worried, waved her hands about in the space around her. 'I was *here*, Signora, all the time. I stopped for a little pasta and wine, and then

I was busy making meal for tonight. See.' She went to the refrigerator and took out a huge fruit salad. 'Then I make the gateau because tomorrow I have busy day and-'

'Didn't you say Signor Taggart called?' Mary interrupted. Cathy reached for the cups as Ginette, her expression worried, said, 'Si. Right in the middle of making gateau the bell rings,' she threw up her hands in exasperation. 'Almost I did not go down, then I thought it might be important; and Signora you would have wanted me to answer, I know this, so I wash my 'ands and go to see who it is calling at siesta time. And he is so – how you say – impatient, that Signor Taggart. He rings again, and again before I reach door.'

'When you said we were not here, Ginette. What did Signor Taggart do then?'

He came into the hall and he asked when you would be back, what time. He...'

'Yes,' Mary said encouragingly.

'He make me cross, Signora, because he pretend I do not understand him and he make *fun*. Not nice fun. He keep pointing to watch on his wrist and shouting and waving his arms, and I – I tell him, "you do not shout at me. I speak the English well and I know what you are saying."

Cathy poured three cups of tea and quietly passed them round, while Mary continued her gentle examination.

'What did Signor Taggart do then Ginette. Did he apologise?'

'He waves his arms about and he come close to me and take my wrist, but I have no watch on *because I am making the gateau*,' her voice rose indignantly, 'and I shake him away Signora, and he walk to the door. Then he come back and say he will telephone later.'

'Then he left?' Mary queried softly.

'Si Signora.' Ginette sipped her tea appreciatively for a few seconds then she looked across to her employer. 'He drop some books he is carrying. Not *your* books Signora, I look as he pick them up.'

Cathy smiled at the mental picture of the loyal Ginette, already angry because Grant was patronising to her, yet not too much so to check on the authorship of the books he dropped.

'Well we had better get in touch with the police again,' Mary said, 'I'll phone them when I've drunk my tea.'

Two members of the polizia arrived and examined the open drawers. They made notes, asked questions, made more notes, before eventually departing. When Ginette had shown them out she returned to the kitchen to cook their meal.

'Fifteen minutes, Signora, will that be all right? It is prepared and will not take long to be ready, and the fruit salad also.'

'Don't worry Ginette. Neither of us are in a rush this evening. We will have a drink while you are doing it, so relax, everything is fine.'

'Dear Ginette,' she said to Cathy as she poured them each a sherry, 'she does like things to run on time. She's been with me so long, yet still she worries in case she doesn't please.'

The telephone rang as Cathy took her first sip. 'Shall I get it?' she asked.

'Thank you.' It was Grant. 'Cathy,' he said, 'how are you?'

'Fine Grant thank you. Why?'

'Well you were unhappy last night, weren't you? You cried.'

She had almost forgotten. 'I'm all right,' she said, 'and you?'

'OK. Do you think I could speak to Mrs Fielding for a moment, Cathy? Oh and will you have supper with me on Saturday. At my place,' he added quickly, 'I don't believe you've been here yet.'

Surprised, she said, 'I'd love to. What's the address Grant?'

'I'll collect you,' he said. She went to fetch her aunt, and wondered about the invitation as she sat waiting for Mary to return. It should be interesting to see where and how Grant lived. At first she had accepted his comments on his lifestyle without question, but lately she had thought his behaviour sometimes mysterious. Not drastically so, yet slightly puzzling as Mary had intimated when they last talked of him. And it was odd the way he clammed up when she asked in the friendliest way if he had heard anymore from the police about his wallet.

She smiled at Mary as she re-entered the room. 'Apparently Grant called lunch time to ask if I would read what he has written so far in this novel he's doing. Very diffident he sounded, not like he is when he comes here.' She reached for her drink, her short, but beautifully shaped and manicured hands holding the Waterford crystal with appreciation.

'Did you agree?'

'Yes. His book might give me a lead on him.'

Cathy shook with laughter, and Mary joined in. 'I'm sorry dear. I didn't mean to sound disparaging. It's that I simply cannot place him, if you see what I mean? He's often charming, mostly charming in fact, but I want to find the element that is eluding me.' Her blue eyes darkened with enthusiasm and interest, 'Quite likely it is a pleasant one, but there's something I haven't fathomed yet, and it's beginning to fascinate me.'

They went out after their meal and walked by the canal, mingling with the tourists in the sweet scented night, and Cathy pushed away all the thoughts of Scott which kept intruding, and tried to concentrate instead on Grant and his sudden invitation to supper at his place.

They turned away from the Grand Canal and over a little bridge. Here the water gently lapped against the tall terracotta buildings, and as they paused in the centre of the bridge a gondola came into view and Mary said, 'Certain material objects have romance woven into them, don't they? For me its old mansions, silver photograph frames, and gondolas.'

Cathy looked down at the sleek, dark shape before it glided beneath the bridge, and her reply strangled in her throat, for of the two people in the gondola, one, a slim blonde young girl, was a stranger to her – the other was Scott Underwood.

CHAPTER 10

Grant came to see Mary the following evening. He brought with him the first two chapters of his novel and a synopsis.

'A rather rough one I'm afraid, but most of the story is in my head. Still it will give you an idea, and I'd like to know if it is worth continuing.'

At Mary's request Cathy stayed downstairs. 'I don't intend to check each stage of his book,' she said, 'and I should be interested in your opinion too. Anyway, aren't you curious to see what it's about?'

Her eyes seemed to dance and Cathy laughed. 'Yes, I am.' Mary poured them all a drink, then suggested that Cathy and Grant sit on the balcony and chat while she read through the first chapter. 'Then we won't disturb each other. I'm a fast reader, but I need to be alone.'

They talked quietly, each sitting on a cushion in the white ironwork chairs which Cathy admired. It wasn't a wide balcony, but spacious enough for four chairs and a small matching table. Cathy placed her drink on the table and turned to smile at Grant.

'What is your book about, and what is it called?'

'It's title is *Pink Elephants* and it's a thriller. Set in Venice of course,' he added.

'I shall miss all this when we return to England,' Cathy said a few moments later as they looked down onto the picturesque scene below.

'What will you do when you go home?'

'Look for another job I suppose. How about you?'

'Not sure yet. I'm solvent for a few more months, then, like you, it will be back to the grindstone I suppose.'

'Unless your book is a best seller,' she said. His laugh rang out, 'Unlikely but a nice thought. Actually I don't think it's too bad, but a book, I'm discovering, is quite a different cup of tea from travel articles. For one thing it's pretty time consuming. I'm not sure I could stick it out until the end, I lose interest quickly.'

'Well, Mary will give you an honest opinion, but I think it would be a shame not to have a go at completing it. After all you can't drift from one thing to another all your life.'

'I should have been born to money,' he said, grinning, 'that's what I'm best at really, travelling and living it up, and you need cash for both those activities.'

Mary called them in when she had read one chapter. 'All right if Cathy looks too Grant?' she asked, 'she's a good critic.'

'Yes, of course.'

'The first chapter's promising. You've set your scene well and you have the action going quickly-' The ringing of the telephone interrupted her and Cathy jumped up.

'I'll get it if you like, then you can continue,' she said to Mary. Scott's rich voice lifted her heart to the stars and she gripped the telephone ledge hard in her determination not to feel carried away.

'Cathy, is Mary there? No need to fetch her to the phone. Just ask if I may come over and see her.'

'She's busy.'

She heard his voice tighten. 'In that case may I speak to her myself please?'

'She has someone with her Scott.'

'For crying out loud what is going on? I know you think I'm suspicious and all that, but it is important that I speak to your aunt, so will you please either fetch her to the telephone or give her a message.'

'I'll see if it's convenient,' she said. She laid the receiver down, took a deep breath and returned to Mary and Grant. 'It's for you, Mary,' she said. As the two women passed each other across the room there was a questioning look in Mary's eyes.

Cathy sat down next to Grant. 'Well, what is the verdict?'

'To finish it and try it out with a publisher or an agent if I can get one. Now let's talk about us Cathy, that's more interesting.'

They all had another drink when Mary returned, and for the next three quarters of an hour the talk was about writing, and about writing the detective thriller in particular. When Grant left Mary looked seriously at her niece.

'Cathy, may I ask you a very personal question, dear?'

'I guess so.'

'Are you in love with Grant Taggart?'

Cathy wasn't sure what she had expected, but her aunt's softly spoken query certainly hadn't entered her head. Yet she knew Mary well enough now to know that she would have a good reason for asking, and she did not know how to answer. The silence between them seemed to last a long while, until Mary said, 'It is presumptuous of me I know, but it is also important to me Cathy.'

'I don't think I'm in love with anyone Mary. It's too soon after Steve.'

'Good, that's good.' Mary stood up. 'Well I'm for bed.'

'But, Mary, don't I get to know the reason for that question?'

'I suppose you're entitled to that.' Mary smiled ruefully at her. 'Grant Taggart has another name. He is also known as Colin Packster. That in itself is not a crime, but it is odd, wouldn't you say?'

'Probably a reasonable explanation. Have you asked Grant?'

'No, not yet.'

'I suppose,' Cathy said, trembling a little inside herself, 'that Scott gave you this piece of information this evening.'

Mary nodded and her white curls bobbed gently with the movement.

'Apart from the fact that he could be quite wrong, which thought I've no doubt hasn't entered his head, what significance does Scott place on this discovery?'

'First, the thought that he could be wrong has entered his head Cathy, which is why he wants us to keep our knowledge of this other name to ourselves just now. Secondly, I didn't ask him the significance of this because Grant was sitting on the other side of the door from the telephone, and it could have produced an awkward few moments.'

'Scott Underwood has it in for Grant, Mary. Ever since he saw Grant kissing me the other evening.'

'You think it's jealousy on Scott's part?'

'Yes.'

'You could be right, but I think Scott is too much of a professional to play games like that. Anyway until he has delved a little more...'

Cathy pressed her lips tightly together to stop any further words. She did not want to quarrel with her aunt who had, she knew, thought from the moment they met that Scott could do no wrong. Yet she wasn't going to stand by and see another man's character discredited when he had no chance to defend himself.

They went to bed, but for Cathy it was not to sleep. If Grant Taggart also had another name she was sure he had a reason for it, a lawful reason. In the short while she had known him he had sometimes been unpredictable, but so had Scott Underwood. That didn't make a man a criminal, and no matter how badly Scott wanted to find the 'master mind' behind this gang he talked about, she didn't think it likely that it would be a man living and working openly in the city for a year, as Grant was.

Cathy didn't see either Grant or Scott for the next few days, and Mary's novel gathered momentum and kept them busy. On Friday she received two letters from home, one from her mother and one from Linda. Her mother chronicled almost every happening of the street during the time she had been away, except the one that interested her most – Steve's marriage. Perhaps she feels it will hurt me too much, and yet I feel so remote from it all now, Cathy thought as she read the letter.

The one from Linda never mentioned Steve this time, but concentrated on office affairs and Linda's own social life.

Cathy wore an ice blue cotton dress for her date with Grant on Saturday evening. Since Scott's telephone call and Mary's question as to how deeply involved she was with Grant Taggart, they had not discussed what she called in her own mind, 'the phantom gang.'

Cathy did not think Mary was avoiding the subject deliberately, it was simply that there was nothing further to say or do about it. The police had not found out who had entered the flat the lunchtime they were out and Ginette was making the gateau. Yet it must have been during those two hours that the disturbance occurred.

Grant telephoned her on Friday evening to invite Mary to supper also. 'I should have mentioned it before, Cathy,' he said, 'and I hope your aunt will forgive such short notice.'

But Mary said she was going to Betty and Guys. 'Do please thank him, and tell him I have another engagement,' she said.

'That's fine. I didn't like to think of her on her own, that's all. I'll see you about seven tomorrow Cathy. Till then,' he blew a kiss into the telephone.

Grant was early, fifteen minutes early, and he came in to wait. Mary offered him a drink, but he refused and they chatted until Cathy came downstairs.

'What does Ginette do when you are both out. She has no-one to cook for,' he said conversationally as they went out.

'She has many friends here, and of course sometimes, like when we were at Garda, she goes home for the weekend.'

'Of course. Your aunt is lucky to find such a good housekeeper.'

'Ginette has been with her for years, she's a real gem. A marvellous cook among all her other talents. She says she will teach me Italian, but I seem to spend a lot of time out in the evenings.' She smiled, almost flirtatiously at him, and he took her hand and said softly, 'Isn't this preferable to sitting indoors on a Saturday evening struggling with another language, my sweet?'

They went by water bus to Grant's apartment. 'I've rented it from a friend for the summer,' he said, 'it's small but convenient.'

'And is he not in Venice?' she asked.

'Sometimes. He flits about a lot. He's not there this evening,' he said, giving her hand a squeeze and smiling, 'and I've prepared a cold supper which I hope you'll enjoy.'

'I'm sure I shall,' she responded to the pressure of his hand in hers as the crowded boat chugged its way along the canal.

The apartment overlooked a small canal and from the window she could see one of the humpty bridges and she wondered if she had actually walked this way on that first afternoon's exploring in Venice. It was possible for she walked a long way and over many small bridges similar to this one.

'Here, let me take your shawl.' Grant draped the black silk garment over his arm. 'Want to see over? It isn't large.'

She followed him into a small bedroom, 'bathroom is next door,' he said, opening the door for a glimpse of a maroon coloured suite, 'then there's a kitchen and a lounge/diner.'

The kitchen proved to be of a reasonable size, and the lounge held a dining table and chairs near the window, three small armchairs, a dresser and a coffee table.

'It's lovely,' she said. The table was set for two with a white cloth, gleaming silver, and sparkling wine glasses. He held a chair out for her. 'I've been looking forward to this evening Cathy, and, just between us, I'm glad your aunt is out tonight. I didn't like to think of her alone there, but I'm glad it's just us two this evening.'

He poured the wine, then disappeared into the kitchen to fetch the meal, which turned out to be a colourful salad. They talked about Italy, and Venice in particular, and afterwards they washed up together in the kitchen. Grant poured two brandies and when she was settled in one of the deep armchairs back in the lounge he said softly, 'I won't be long. I have one telephone call to make, a business one.' He closed the door quietly and she picked up her glass and swirled the golden liquid around. It had been a perfect evening. Was she in love with Grant Taggart? She liked him very much, and tonight they had seemed so in tune with each other. Tentatively she sipped her drink before holding it once more to let the fiery flow warm her vision. She could hear Grant's voice outside in the hall and she wondered who he could be telephoning this time of night on business. She had risen and was looking out of the window and down towards the still waters of the canal when he returned.

'Everything all right?' she asked

'Everything's fine,' he said. 'Sorry about that, I don't usually mix business with pleasure, but this chap was only available late this evening. Now we can continue to enjoy ourselves. You are enjoying yourself Cathy, aren't you?' He took her in his arms and she surrendered to his kisses.

It was over an hour later when he took her home. As they approached the door she saw the policeman standing there. He put out a restraining hand and spoke rapidly in Italian. Grant translated for her. 'He wants to know who you are and why you are going in here,' he told her.

Within minutes it was established that she lived here, and the policeman stood aside to let them enter. They took the stairs two at a time, and almost bumped into another member of the polizia in the hall by the lift.

'What has happened, what is going on?' Cathy cried, and then Mary came out of the lounge and they fell into each other's arms.

'It's all right,' Mary said, 'we had burglars again and Scott was tied up but he's OK. He's not hurt at all.'

Scott was in the room sitting on the sofa with a drink in his hands. She rushed towards him, then stopped, suddenly self-conscious, remembering their last meeting.

'Scott,' she said, 'Scott, are you sure you're all right?'

'Perfectly,' he answered, except for my temper. If I could get my hands on those bastards.'

They sat on after the polizia had left, telling Cathy and Grant what had happened. 'I didn't see who hit me, but there was more than one involved because just before I passed out I heard them talking, and I'm sure there were three different voices.'

Cathy, who had sat down next to Scott on the sofa asked quietly, 'Did they take anything?'

'Mary's jewel box.'

Grant, who had been quiet throughout most of their exchanges said now, 'I guess I had better be getting back.' He looked across to Mary. 'I am sorry Mrs Fielding. Was there – was there much of great value in it?'

'Everything was of great sentimental value,' Mary said thickly, 'and yes, there was monetary value as well.'

Grant walked over to her. 'I hope they catch them. If there is anything I can do, please don't hesitate to ask.' He nodded briefly to Scott, then turning to Cathy said, 'It's OK, I'll see myself out, don't bother to come down again.'

Ginette came in from the kitchen carrying a tray. 'I've made us all a nice cup of tea,' she said, 'I know that is what Signora Maria would like.' She saw Cathy and the smile left her face, 'Ah, Signorina, it is terrible, terrible. I come home from meeting some friends and find Signor Underwood in here tied up and with the scarf over his mouth – ah Signorina it was awful...'

'Poor Ginette discovered the break-in,' Mary said. 'Ah, thank you,' she took a cup of tea from the tray and smiled at her housekeeper, 'just what we all need, Ginette.'

As they drank so Mary and Scott filled Cathy in on the events of the past few hours. How Scott had been sitting reading and left the room to go to the bathroom, returning to be knocked out and tied up and blindfolded without even seeing his captors.

'I curse myself for that slip,' he said, looking at Mary, 'but I swear they are the quietest burglars I've ever known. They must have a key because there was no forced entry, but if I had been here where I ought to have been, I would probably have heard something.'

'No point blaming yourself Scott. I'm simply thankful you weren't hurt,' Mary said. Cathy drank some of her tea, then, taking a deep breath she looked into Scott's velvety eyes and asked the question that was puzzling her.

'How was it that you were here in the first place, Scott?'

'A hunch. When I realised nobody would be in this evening – Mary said Ginette had gone to visit friends, you were out, and she was with Betty and Guy, I suggested my vigil. And if I hadn't gone into the bathroom, and that noisy cistern alerting them to the fact that someone else was in the house...'

Cathy found she was trembling as she thought of three men pouncing on Scott, and her concern made her say sharply, 'It was foolish to be here alone if you had any inkling something might happen.'

'I didn't. Not anything definite. I told you it was just a hunch, but if only I had been here in this room, sitting quite still without lights on, I would have heard them coming I reckon. My ears are pretty sharp, and I would have had the element of surprise instead of them.'

Cathy turned away, partly to avoid him seeing the emotion she knew must show on her face. Oh Scott, Scott, she moaned silently, while I was out enjoying myself, you were here in danger, guarding Mary's jewels.

He finished his tea and rose. 'Better be getting back, Mary. I'll probably see you tomorrow sometime, when Guy and Betty know what happened they're bound to come over.'

Guy had brought Mary home, but because it was late, had not come up with her, but simply seen her to the lift.

'These men,' Cathy said, 'came in the back way I gather.'

'Yes.' Scott eased his hand round his jaw.

'Do you think that might indicate they live close?'

'Not necessarily. They left by boat. I heard the lift go down and the engine of the craft start up, but the police are convinced they entered through the back door and in fact had a key.'

'Thank God Scott wasn't badly injured,' Mary said when he had gone, 'I'd never have forgiven myself for agreeing. One thing, it knocks Grant Taggart from his list of suspects because we know where he was all evening.'

Cathy felt the colour ebbing from her cheeks, and Mary said, 'Sorry Cathy, I didn't mean to hurt, but Scott and I had both wondered about him.'

'I didn't realise,' Cathy said slowly, 'although I suppose I should have done. You checked on him the other evening, with that different name. Well Grant was with me all the time.'

Mary stood up and swayed a little, and Cathy hurried over. 'You're done in, let me help you to bed.' Suddenly Mary did look her age, but she stopped to say goodnight to Ginette before she went upstairs.

'Ginette was untying Scott when I got in,' she said as she turned to go into her room, 'and the thugs had been left about an hour, so they could be miles away by now.'

Cathy kissed her aunt gently on the cheek. 'Try to sleep,' she said, 'and maybe the police will have a lead by the morning.'

CHAPTER 11

Mary said to Ginette when she served breakfast, the traditional English breakfast of egg, bacon and tomato, for Sunday morning, 'I have a favour to ask you, Ginette.'

'Signora,'

'That you do not mention the robbery to anyone for a time. Signor Underwood thinks it best.'

Cathy saw the disappointment in Ginettes eyes, and silently sympathised.

'Si, Signora, I will not say *one* word. It will not be easy, but to no-one will I tell how I find Signor Underwood all tied up.'

'Thank you Ginette.'

Cathy sat on her balcony writing letters home during the morning, and not even to her mother did she mention the missing jewels. Betty and Guy had telephoned early and it was agreed that they all met for lunch. She found she could hardly wait to see Scott again and be sure he was having no ill effects from being knocked out.

The canal traffic was busy and she let her thoughts wander back to the evening she and Mary had seen Scott in the gondola with the golden haired girl. Who was she? A holidaymaker – a friend of Betty and Guy. She looked English more than Italian, and they had been sitting side by side in the gondola without touching, but that meant nothing. If she was on holiday Scott may have only met her a short time before, too soon maybe for hand holding, even in that most romantic of carriages, a gondola.

Her enormous concern for Scott last night had surprised her, and the relief that he wasn't injured had been quickly followed by irritation because of his interference. Her feelings for him were double edged; always it seemed the one superseding the other. Sighing deeply Cathy tried again to concentrate on the letter she was writing, but it was no use. Scott's image kept forcing its way between the pad and her thoughts. Tears welled in her eyes as she remembered his scathing remarks about gondolas, 'The most expensive way to see Venice,' and remembered the blonde sitting demurely by his side in one. Foolish to dream, even more so where Scott was concerned because they almost always quarrelled after only a short while together.

Unbidden, the memory of the magical weekend on Garda pushed itself to the front of her mind. That was when she first realised that she loved him, yet since then they had quarrelled again, and anyway she told herself as she angrily brushed the tell-tale wetness from her eyes, he has a girlfriend, the slim blonde who was riding under the bridges of Venice with him so recently. Then there was the worrying business of Mary's jewels. She didn't like to discuss the possibilities of getting them back with her aunt too much, and adding to her stress. She wondered what the chances of recovering them were, yet if she mentioned it to Scott it might not be received in the right spirit, as he so obviously felt it was his fault for not being in a position to surprise the thieves. Yet what could he have done against three men?

A tiny spurt of anger quickened inside her, at the thought that he should put himself into a position of such danger. With his job surely he ought to know better. That over-sized ego wanting to do it all by himself. Yet as fast as the idea came so she now dismissed it, for in the last few weeks she had realised that Scott's enthusiasm was for a good job of work well done. His nature would not allow him to leave the place unprotected while his instincts and calculations told him the gang were ready to strike and simply awaiting an opportunity. She also thought he may know more than he had told any of them. Yet he didn't know *who* they were, and in spite of the other evening, he still had not seen their faces.

'The classic trick,' he told them bitterly, 'someone waiting behind the door as I came in. I never saw who hit me, and when I came round I was trussed up and bound round the eyes. Gagged too until they left. They freed my mouth then, but apart from the comfort, it offered no practical use because no-one outside would hear cries for help from the flat unless you were on the balcony, and I was tied to the chair.'

Cathy finished her final letter and went indoors in search of her aunt. Mary looked rather drawn, she still had her lovely rosy cheeks, Cathy couldn't remember a time when her aunt looked pale for more than a few seconds, but there was pain in her eyes this morning and Cathy longed to be able to offer some solution, put forward an idea that would help.

Mary herself broached the subject of the stolen jewellery box. 'They are all insured,' she said, 'and I suppose there is the chance they will be recovered. Trouble is there isn't anything so distinctive and unusual that it would cause raised eyebrows to sell.'

'They've probably got a 'fence' lined up,' Cathy said. Mary nodded. 'I expect so. They are likely to be in Rome now, that's the most logical place I would think.'

'What are the police doing?'

'They don't say. Well only that they have issued a list of the missing items. The only ones we have saved are these,' she held out a hand that was very slightly trembling, and displayed her diamond engagement ring and a beautiful opal surrounded with tiny rubies and diamonds.

'I was wearing these two that evening. And of course the lovely emerald. Thank heaven I gave it to you last week Cathy or we would have lost that one too.'

Tears filled her eyes and she brushed them away impatiently. 'Scott and I have tried to work out how the gang came to know about the collection, and so far we haven't come up with anything concrete. He thinks it was planned for that night and that the other intrusions were simply reconnaissances. What do you think?'

'I have been wondering why, on that second occasion, they didn't find them. The first time they couldn't because you had the box with you when we went to Lake Garda, but that next time when they obviously did over your drawer, I can't understand.'

'Scott says they were disturbed.'

Cathy looked sharply at her aunt, 'You and Scott seem to have discussed the situation pretty thoroughly.'

'Yes, we have. He says he saw someone hanging about that lunchtime.'

Cathy shrugged. 'It's a bit vague, isn't it?' she said, 'I mean, I expect there were several people in the piazza at that time of day. I noticed one or two myself when we went out.'

'He says that one of the people who were hanging about that lunchtime was Grant Taggart.' Mary spoke quite slowly and very softly.

Cathy jumped to Grant's defence. 'That doesn't make him involved. Scott himself must have been 'hanging about' and anyone watching may have thought he was up to no good. I don't see-'

'You wanted to be completely in the picture and now you are,' Mary said decisively, 'I agree it doesn't mean Grant has any ulterior motive, but we have to consider all possibilities dear, and we know very little about the man.'

'It's ridiculous. Why would Grant want to steal your collection anyway? He doesn't need the money. I told you he recently had a legacy from his uncle which has enabled him to take a year off to write his novel.'

They looked at each other and Mary laughed nervously, 'It's a case of elimination,' she said.

'And alibi,' Cathy ventured, 'and I can vouch for Grant the night of the robbery.'

Cathy was still cross as they went to their rendezvous. Scott niggled and niggled once he got an idea into his head, and –

'There's Grant now,' Mary's voice cut into her seething thoughts, and looking across the piazza, Cathy saw him coming towards them.

'My telephone is out of order so I thought I would call and see if you are free this evening, Cathy,' he said after greeting them both.

Her smile was radiant. 'Yes, I am.'

'All right if I pick you up about seven?'

'Fine, I'll look forward to it.'

He looked surprised at the enthusiasm in her voice, then, lowering his tone almost reverently he asked Mary if there had been any progress regarding the robbery.

'None, but it's early days yet Grant,' she said.

Betty, Guy, and Scott were waiting for them at the arranged meeting place. As Scott fell into step beside her she tried, unsuccessfully to fight the surge of joy that leapt through her veins. Why could he make her feel like this? The last thing she expected, or wanted during this trip to Venice was emotional complications. Yet she couldn't deny to herself the excitement he generated with his presence, and as his hand brushed hers as they walked along, she tried not to let him see the effect it had on her.

Grant was so nice, so elegant and gentle even, yet his kisses never left her mouth tingling for more, his arm around her never gave her the feeling that she was flying instead of walking.

'Cathy, I don't believe you have listened to one word...' They reached the café, and as he stood aside for her to enter she murmured, 'Sorry, my mind was going over the events of last evening, and wondering about the people who knew we were all going to be out.'

They settled themselves at a table, and under cover of the menu Scott said, 'And have you come up with anyone?'

'No, have you?'

'I'm working on it.' His voice was quiet, but his tone was sharp. Cathy enjoyed the meal, and knew now that her verbal sparring with Scott was a form of protection. First against her feelings for him, and now against the knowledge that, in spite of his kisses when they were in Gargnano, they had not meant more than a brief attraction because they were thrown together. The chemistry of two young people in a sunny and romantic clime. It was a well-known fact that emotions flourished in the warmer hemisphere, that was why the Latins were such an exuberant and volatile race, while in the colder regions maybe the atmosphere did have repercussions on the hearts and minds of the inhabitants, she thought. Suddenly she had to fight her tears. No, this wasn't how she wanted it to be. She loved Scott, for better or worse, despite the way they sparked each other off with their quick reactions. However it was for him, for her it was more than a flirtation, more than the chemistry of two young bodies, more, much more than a bottle of wine and dinner for two, and a walk home beneath a canopy of silver stars in a deep velvet sky.

'Cathy, are you all right, love?'

She blinked away the offending tears before they fell. 'Yes, of course. I'm trying to study the menu,' she said, and cursed herself for not being able to tell him, 'I love you Scott and I'm madly jealous of the blonde in the gondola with you.'

After lunch they walked for a while by the Grand Canal, went into St Mark's Square and simply gazed at the beauty and agelessness of it all, and then they went their separate ways, Mary and Cathy saying their farewells at the door or their apartment, and laughing sadly when Scott asked if he should come upstairs with them. 'No need dear, there is nothing left to steal now,' Mary said.

Cathy was ready when Grant rang the bell at seven, and giving Mary a quick kiss on the top of her head as she sat in her chair reading the inevitable detective story, she went downstairs to meet him. It was a pleasant evening and a nice enough meal. Grant was attentive but not a nuisance, and when they walked home and he slipped an arm round her waist she snuggled up to him and they kissed, passionately on his part, and tenderly on hers. When he wanted to linger she excused herself because she had to rise early the next morning. 'For me Monday starts a working week, for you –'

'I'm working too Cathy, on my novel.'

'Yes, but you can make your own time, well, to an extent,' she amended.

'Goodnight lovely Cathy, I'll phone you soon.' He paused, his hand still holding tightly to hers. 'You'll let me know any developments about the robbery,' he whispered, 'I feel so terribly sorry for your aunt, all those lovely gems.'

Although she was tired it took Cathy a long while to go to sleep. She could not erase from her mind the pictures of Grant as he voiced his concern for Mary, and Scott as he methodically checked alibis and exonerated yet another suspect from his list. I know it is what a policeman has to do, but I wonder how he would react if suddenly I appeared on that list, she thought. Maybe I am on it – niece covets aunt's gems – attractive young detective denounces her. As her laughter at the idea broke forth it changed rapidly to harsh, dry sobs, and Cathy turned her face into the pillow to stifle them. Damn Scott Underwood and his bloody efficiency.

CHAPTER 12

Mary and Cathy visited Maria, the young woman whose labour pains had begun at Mary's party. They went latish on Monday afternoon, and after admiring the solemn, dark eyed baby, Maria took them on a tour of the house and introduced them to her mother. Over tea Maria laughed a little about the evening young Giovanni was born.

'Spaventare, terrificare.'

'Frightened, terrified,' Mary translated softly for Cathy, 'when the man came in.'

Mary, a cup halfway to her mouth, stopped and said slowly, 'What man, Maria?'

Maria looked surprised. 'Was with you,' she said, looking at Cathy, 'he came for your…' she paused, searching for the word, then triumphantly pulled a handkerchief from the pocket of her skirt.

'He was not with Cathy when he came in,' Mary asked quietly, raising her voice slightly towards the last words.

'No, Signora.'

'Why, and how did he frighten you?' Mary's voice was gently coaxing.

Maria's beautiful dark eyes widened and she laid a hand across her stomach. 'The pain, Signora. I did not see him come in. I look up from bad pain when it goes and I see him in mirror. He – he tell me he look for fazzoletto, but he – he frighten me he look so angry.'

'What did he look like, Maria? Dark,' Mary indicated Maria's own hair, 'or like Cathy?'

Maria shook her head. 'I do not remember. The pain you see. He ran past me when I screamed.' The expression in her eyes softened, 'then you come Signora, and you help me.'

Grant or Scott, Cathy asked herself as they returned home. She remembered how Scott had startled her when she had gone in to fetch Maria's handbag – his hand over her mouth, and his anger when he found it was her. Had there been someone else prowling around on the night of the party. Had it been Grant?

'Was with you,' Maria had said, but she hadn't spent all her time with Grant. At stages they had both been with her. Mary's voice broke into her sombre thoughts. 'A funny business, isn't it Cathy? If only Maria could recall what he looked like, but I believe her when she says she doesn't. The poor child was panic stricken and in great pain. All that registered was his anger obviously. But Cathy, anger at not finding the box, or at suddenly realising someone was in the room. I wonder which?'

'It would have been a risky business with so many people in the house, even if he had located them,' Cathy said.

'Not necessarily. He could have taken the gems out of the box and slipped them into his pocket. A lot of them anyway. We wouldn't have discovered the theft until after the party when I was putting my necklace and ring away, or even the following morning if I had been too tired and left them on the dressing table overnight.'

'I suppose so,' Cathy said reluctantly, 'but then the police would have had to grill everyone and...'

Mary shook her head, 'I believe, looking at the situation now, that I would have dismissed the idea that it could have been anyone at the party. I would have thought an outsider had come in, and under cover of the noise made his haul. Or hers.'

Cathy stopped walking and said in surprise, 'You think it might have been a woman?'

'It's possible, but no, not now. Not since Scott was tied up. But I am convinced that the men who did that and took the box were working for someone else. That's who we want, the ringleader. And he, or she, has kept a very low profile and been operating this gang for some time now according to Scott. He thinks the brains behind it is in Venice.'

They resumed their walk towards home. 'You and Scott obviously discuss this frequently,' Cathy remarked.

'Yes.' There was silence for a few moments, and then Mary said, 'I'm glad it didn't happen at the party because you are right, the police would have *had* to question everyone and that would have been awful. Most of the people who were there are my friends. We must tell Scott about Maria's revelation this afternoon.'

'Suppose it was Scott who startled her?'

'Scott.'

'Well, he was with me during the evening. Quite a lot, he and Grant were. Maria seemed to think it was one of them, although I did in fact talk to and sit with various others during the party, but I suppose they were the only unattached ones there.' As they turned into the entrance to the apartment Mary said quietly, 'We will tell them both – together. I'll invite them here one evening and I will casually mention Maria's remark. It will be interesting to see the reactions don't you think?'

Cathy wasn't sure. She could not believe that either of them had anything to do with a gang of thieves, yet someone was masterminding an operation that had so far successfully pulled off several coups according to Scott.

'Perhaps it is best left to the police, Mary. Anyway I daresay whoever disturbed Maria in the bedroom did have a good reason for being there. She probably startled him as much as he did her when he realised she was there. And,' she added quickly, 'Maria could be mistaken about seeing him searching in the drawer. She was, on her own admission, in a bit of a state.'

'I've thought of that, yet she did not imagine someone else in the room. She actually saw a man through the mirror on the dressing table. That's what startled her so, because she hadn't heard him come in.'

'And he hadn't seen her, huddled up in pain amongst the shawls and bags on the bed,' Cathy said thinking aloud. 'So when will you invite Scott and Grant round?'

'I may not yet. It's just a thought. For the moment shall we keep our own council dear?'

Mary worked steadily on her book during the following week, and Cathy had little time for her own thoughts or dreams. The story was flowing and she suspected that Mary found it kept her mind away from the loss of her wonderful collection of gems. She had loved her aunt before, now she loved and admired her, for Mary displayed a quiet courage at the loss of the tangible evidence of her memories. During the time they had worked together Mary told Cathy several stories about the collection.

'That necklace we bought when *The Golden Ladder* was published,' she said, displaying a beautiful rope of gold links, 'and that opal ring was after *Fire In My Heart*...'Cathy knew that, although the monetary loss was substantial and not lightly dismissed, the real heartache was the love Mary had for her jewels and the memories they evoked.

She saw Scott early one evening in San Marco. He was alone, on the opposite side of the square, and as she watched his purposeful figure striding along she wondered what had become of the fair haired girl. She knew she was foolish to be so upset by that sighting. After all Scott, as far as she knew, was free to indulge in friendships and trysts as much as he wanted. Yet the memory of an evening on Garda when they talked and kissed as lovers do was strong in her. Damn you Scott – I will not let you make me miserable, she thought.

When Grant telephoned on Friday to ask her out for a meal she accepted, and when Mary suggested that she invite him round for a drink on Saturday evening she agreed, although not enthusiastically.

They walked for a while, along by the canal. 'I may have to fly back to London soon Cathy,' Grant said as they swung along beside the grey waters. 'I'll be back though. Bit of family trouble. I'm hoping I can avoid going, and sort it out from here, but that may not be possible.

Anyway I should only be gone about a week or ten days at the most, you will still be here when I return, won't you?'

They went into a restaurant they had liked before, in a little piazza, and after they had ordered he said earnestly, 'How is your aunt. Have they caught anyone or recovered her jewels yet?'

Her face flushed as she remembered why she was going to invite him to the flat on Saturday. 'No, we've heard nothing,' she answered truthfully, adding quickly, 'but I do have a message for you from my aunt. She said would you come along for a drink tomorrow evening Grant?'

He looked surprised. 'Is it a party?'

'N-no. I think she is asking one or two others. Just a friendly drink,' she finished lamely. She thought for a moment he was going to refuse, then he sat upright in the chair and said, 'That is very nice of her. I should like to come Cathy. What time?'

'About seven she said.'

'I'll be there. Ah, here comes our food.'

The rest of the evening passed pleasantly enough, and before he left her at the entrance to the apartment Grant pulled her into his arms and beginning with rough hungry kisses, gradually became tenderer, until releasing her gently he said, 'Will you miss me if I have to go to London Cathy, or is superman still in the offing?'

'Don't be silly Grant. I told you at the start I'm not interested in any serious relationship.'

He made a sound that could have been a laugh, and pressed her hard against him. 'You're so lovely my sweet.

You're a wonderful bonus and it would be so easy to get carried away.' Releasing her abruptly he pushed her towards the entrance, 'Until tomorrow evening,' he said, and hurried off.

The combination of very hard work, good food and much wine ensured sleep and when she woke on Saturday morning it was almost an hour later than usual. Ah well, she told herself, good thing it is Saturday and no work, except some typing up. Mary hadn't promised her an easy ride when she offered the job, and Cathy realised for perhaps the first time how hard her aunt worked for the lifestyle she had. Her mother had sometimes said that it was all right for Mary, gadding off to Venice every year, and often to other countries for a holiday if she made extra sales, but she worked darned hard for it, Cathy thought.

They had been in Venice four months now, and she knew she would have to start looking for a job as soon as she returned home. It would seem strange to live in England again after the romance and excitement of Venice. Strange to wake up in suburbia to the noise of the milkman's electric float rather than to the glory of a Venetian morning, and to go to bed at night to the silence of Tiptonfield rather than the gentle sounds of Italy.

She knew she would always be grateful to Mary for giving her this wonderful chance. Pippa would be back for the next trip, but having now worked for an author maybe she could find another similar job. One thing was certain, it would be away from Tiptonfield if she could manage it. Her mother had coped very well without her and she had no great desire to bump into Steve and his wife. She did not often think about him now, but the years spent knowing him would never be wiped out. So many of her early memories were tied up with his, but she knew beyond doubt now that it would have been wrong for them to marry. She had thought she was in love with Steve, yet it had never been the devastating flood of feeling that she almost drowned in whenever Scott was present. He didn't need to touch her even, before that torrent of emotion tumbled about her like a waterfall, gathering momentum as it cascaded until she found the utter peace and tranquillity of true contentment that followed his kiss.

Cathy typed out the previous days' work and went in search of her aunt. 'Grant is coming round this evening,' she said.

'Good, so is Scott. And Betty and Guy. Should be interesting. You never mentioned Maria to him?'

'Of course not, I thought that was the idea, Scott – Scott isn't in the picture either, is he?'

Mary smiled. 'No. I guess I'm playing detective myself a bit here. As you said yesterday there is probably a good reason why Grant, if it was him, walked over to the drawer and opened it, but I cannot imagine one, unless he was looking for something.'

'On the other hand,' Cathy said, 'Maria's English isn't too hot and maybe she was trying to say he walked over *to* the chest of drawers, and not that he opened it. Was it closed or pulled out when you went to Maria's aid?'

Mary's blue eyes widened. 'I have to admit that I don't know Cathy. And of course nothing was stolen that night…'

They all arrived together. Betty, Guy and Scott at the canal entrance in their boat, and Grant from the piazza at the back. When the greetings were over and they all settled in their chairs with a drink by their sides, they talked about Venice, Italy, England, all impersonal subjects chatted about in a general way. Grant sat next to Cathy on the sofa and once or twice his arm ran along the back, but she never took advantage and laid her head against it. She was aware that from time to time Scott was watching her, his brown eyes looked wary, and she wondered if he was jealous, but she dismissed the idea almost immediately.

After about an hour Ginette appeared, carrying a tray filled with plates of thinly cut sandwiches arranged prettily on crinkled doilies. Mary looked across to Guy, 'Would you see to the drinks for me please,' she asked, and he refilled their glasses.

'Has Cathy told you our latest news,' she said when Guy sat down again. 'The police are well on the track of our robbers.'

Scott turned quickly, looking startled. 'No. Tell us, Mary.'

'Well it was Maria really. You remember Maria who had to be rushed to hospital the night of our party?'

'Yes.' This encouragement came from Scott and Betty, while Guy looked quizzically at Mary, who was obviously enjoying herself now. She looked carefully all-round the room. 'Well the first attempt was made that night and she foiled it. Unwittingly of course,' she spread her hands wide, Italian fashion, 'and the poor child was in such pain and despair she didn't fully realise, but of course now her evidence is vital.'

Cathy felt Grant tense up, but his voice sounded normal enough as he asked, 'She saw someone trying to take the jewels?'

Mary nodded towards him in an elaborately casual fashion. 'Mmm, but with all the excitement of that night, and the thrill of her baby she didn't think about it again. Well of course, at first she didn't *know*, because they weren't actually stolen then.'

'Go on,' said Guy, as she paused dramatically.

Mary shrugged. 'Well that's it really. When she knew about the robbery later she remembered that incident and thought it might be of use to the police.'

The silence was so strong that Cathy could hear Grant breathing as he sat next to her, and into it Mary threw her trump card, 'And of course, it is.'

Cathy noticed that Scott was gazing at Grant, who moved forward slightly and said, 'You mean they've caught them?'

'Not quite Grant, but they're on the right track.' She rose quickly from her chair and went over to the table where Ginette had left the plate of sandwiches. 'Another sandwich anyone? Grant?'

'No thank you. In fact I think I ought to be going soon.'

'So early. I was just going to make some coffee.'

Sitting next to Grant and immediately in front of where her aunt was standing Cathy felt the current of excitement, then Grant said quietly, 'Well maybe one more sandwich with a cup of coffee then. They are delicious, Mrs. Fielding.'

When Mary had gone to the kitchen to ask Ginette about coffee, Scott said, 'That was good news. With Maria's description of one, and my recognition of the other three voices the situation looks fine now. Only thing is they may have already disposed of the booty. What do you think, Grant?'

'Could be. Depends I suppose what sort of contacts they have. I imagine they would want to get rid of it as quickly as possible, wouldn't you in the circumstances, Scott?'

'Oh yes, indeed I would. But have they been able to?'

'I'd be content to leave it to the police I think, they aren't fools.' Grant replied, leaping from his seat as Mary returned and taking the tray from her hands. He left soon afterwards, and Cathy went downstairs to let him out. 'I'll ring you,' he said, 'it may not be for a few days because I might have to go to England as I told you, but I'll be in touch.'

When Cathy returned the others were preparing to leave. Scott held back a little as he reached the door. 'I hope Mary wasn't over playacting,' he said softly, 'we don't want her jewels dumped in the canal.'

'You've a nasty suspicious mind-' she began, but his arm swiftly came round her.

'I know,' he whispered, his pale gold hair close to her copper curls, 'it's the training I've had. Makes a chap notice every little detail. For instance do you know your eyes sometimes glow like that emerald on your finger, and your lips are the most kissable in the world?'

CHAPTER 13

Grant Taggart seems to have disappeared from Venice,' Scott said a few days later when he came in one evening with an invitation to dine with his aunt and uncle the following day.

'He's in England,' she said.

'Is he. How do you know?'

'Oh Scott, the simplest way in the world. Because he told me he was going. You read too much into things.'

'Did he give you an address?'

Her tone now matched his in sharpness. 'Of course not. He had no reason to. In any case he will be returning soon.'

'He told you that too?'

'He did. And before you jump to the conclusion it was to do with the other night, he had told me before he came for drinks. Any more questions?'

They were alone in the drawing room, waiting for Mary, who had gone upstairs to fetch something she wanted him to take to Betty. Moving closer to her he said quietly, 'I'm sorry Cathy. I have to go back myself very shortly and I hoped to return your aunt's jewellery to her and catch the gang before that.'

'I fail to see what Grant's departure for England, *on family business*, has to do with the robbery Scott.' She knew her lip was quivering but it had to be said. 'I know you suspect him of being the leader of this – this gang you say is operating in Europe, but I say he can't be. He was with me the entire evening when they were stolen, he didn't even know us until a few months ago. We all met on the boat coming over, didn't you find that much out?'

'All right, I've said I'm sorry.' Scott moved away and walked over to the balcony. 'I've never suggested he stole them himself Cathy, but someone is running this show. Whoever it is is playing a clever game. So far the gang haven't gone for anything which would be hard to sell, but always for items which will fetch a good price. Makes the risks worthwhile I guess.'

'Do you think I don't want the gang caught too,' Cathy said to his back, 'it's simply that right from the start you have been suspicious about Grant Taggart. I admit I don't know him well, but look at it logically Scott. He has enough money left him in a legacy to enable him to spend a year doing something he has always wanted to do, write a book. It all ties in. Grant was a journalist for some time anyway, so what is more feasible than a book. He chose Venice for his setting, he knows the place, and – and it isn't all a sham Scott. He really is writing a book, not only I, but Mary also has seen the first two chapters.'

Scott turned round and faced her, a strange expression on his face. 'You're not in love with him, are you Cathy?'

'What on earth has that got to do with it? Sometimes you are impossible Scott.' Angrily she moved towards the door, almost bumping into her aunt who was just coming through.

'Sorry I've been so long,' Mary said, 'I stopped to wrap it in some pretty paper I knew I had, but had mislaid.' She handed Scott a package tied with silver ribbon. 'Keep it until tomorrow morning,' she said, 'I do like people to have their gifts on the correct day. Now how about a cool drink. Lemon or orange with ice?'

Cathy waited until she heard Scott leaving before she came downstairs. Mary was sitting on the balcony, an empty glass on the white table beside her.

'Hullo dear. We have an invitation to dine with the Underwood's tomorrow. It's Betty's birthday and she wants to celebrate at home. Only us and one other couple I believe, so it will be a small party. You will come, won't you?'

'Yes, I'd like to.'

'I couldn't help overhearing you and Scott having words,' Mary said. 'He's a very frustrated man at present. Scott hates having nothing to do and he badly wanted to clear up this case. He's taken a personal interest in it because it's us. I mean he always does his best of course, but I think he has taken it more to heart you know.'

'I know,' Cathy said, 'and you were right, we were arguing. We always seem to be either quarrelling or kissing. I don't know what to make of it.'

Mary smiled. 'I have noticed how you react to each other. Possibly because you've both been badly hurt in the past and you are each wary of the other. Scott's arm is almost one hundred per cent again I gather. Has he told you how it was injured, Cathy?'

'No.' Cathy sat down.

'Two chaps in a pub started arguing. One produced a knife, and Scott, who was there with a friend, simply having a quiet drink, got between them and, according to the barman, saved the other chap from being murdered because the knife was aimed at his throat. In the struggle the knife went into Scott's arm. Betty and Guy told me.'

'He wasn't on duty then?'

'No. He had a couple of operations on his arm, and physiotherapy treatment. Apparently he is lucky to have the use of it. Betty says that at first they thought it would be paralysed, or as good as for the purposes of police work.'

It was a pleasant gathering the following evening for Betty's birthday party. There were seven people, Guy, Betty, Scott, Mary and herself, and a couple who ran a wine store in Treviso and were old friends of Betty and Guy. After the excellent meal and the jolly happy birthday toasts Cathy found herself sitting next to Scott on the two seater settee.

'How about another evening out? Strictly pleasure,' he said quickly, 'I promise not to mention,' he leant over and whispered softly in her ear, 'the robbery or anything connected with it.'

She laughed and said brightly, 'Fine, I'll look forward to it.'

How tame that sounded she thought when she recalled the evening much later before she went to bed. Look forward to it, when every little tingle in her body was crying out to be near him. It was such a madness that had got into her, a wild, wonderful feeling that made her more sure than she had ever been of anything in the world that she wanted Scott for her man.

Yet, perversely she fought him, both in her heart and openly. What was it Mary had said earlier, 'You've both been badly hurt in the past.' Did Scott have a broken romance too? She was amazed by the shock of jealousy she felt.

They met and dined again during the week and she returned to Casa Ristori on the edge of the deepest happiness she had felt yet in her twenty three years.

Grant returned at the end of the week. He telephoned on Saturday morning. 'When can I see you Cathy? God, I've missed you.' She marvelled at the emotion in his voice.

'Have you. Did you sort everything out Grant?'

'Oh yes. Listen, how about dinner tonight. At my place. I'll come for you at seven.'

'No I can't,' she said.

'Why not? You're not going anywhere else, are you?'

'Yes.'

'Damn. Sorry my love, it's just that being away has made me realise how much you've come to mean to me. All right, how about tomorrow then?'

'I don't think – ' she began, when he interrupted her.

'Cathy please. I didn't realise, look I can't explain over the phone but I've got to see you. Please Cathy, it's very important to me. How about tomorrow morning. I'll meet you for coffee at, say ten o clock.'

She tried to say no but Grant was persistent and persuasive. 'Why Cathy? Honestly I do need to see you. Surely you can spare an hour out of your day to have a drink with me. Please.'

She finally agreed to meet him on Sunday morning, and smiling quietly to herself she went in search of Mary.

'Have you been in a gondola yet?' Scott asked her on Saturday evening.

'No.' The picture of Scott with the pretty, fair haired girl flashed into her mind's eye.

'Well how about a trip?'

'It's a bit costly,' she said, her voice dancing with happy mischief as she remembered a previous conversation early in their acquaintance.

Scott smiled down at her, 'But worth it for the right girl,' he said softly, and for a moment the brightness in her heart dimmed as she wondered how many he had said similar words to.

Swiftly he bent and kissed the top of her head, and the colours returned, brighter and clearer than before.

It was romantic to glide through the waters of the canals in the graceful gondola, to sit holding hands tightly, to talk to each other with looks rather than words, and Cathy resolutely put the picture of the time she had watched Scott glide beneath the bridge on which she and Mary were standing, out of her mind. He hadn't been as close to that girl, he hadn't been holding her hand, stroking her fingers… when the ride was over they went for a meal, but it wasn't until they were walking home, arms and hands entwined, that he told her he would soon be returning to England.

'Let's have a day out tomorrow Cathy. Where would you like to go? Guy says I can borrow the car, so, your wish is my command.'

'I – I can't manage tomorrow,' she said, 'at least not until the afternoon.'

'Oh Cathy. All right, where would you like to go then?'

'I don't mind Scott. You choose. Surprise me.'

Before they parted that night he arranged to call for her at two o clock on Sunday. 'Lovely Cathy,' he murmured, his lips against her hair. 'You'll be back in England yourself a couple of months after me, there's no-one else is there Cathy? You know I've fallen in love with you.'

Tears of happiness filled her eyes. 'I love you too Scott,' she said, and their lips met again for a long, passionate kiss.

She went to meet Grant the following morning with resentment in her heart. If she had only known Scott would invite her out for the day she would never have agreed to this date. It wasn't in her nature to break it now, but it was annoying to miss precious hours with Scott.

Grant appeared on the dot of ten at the café where they had arranged to meet. She thought he looked tired, and his first words confirmed this. 'I've had a harassing time Cathy and I may have to return and have another go at sorting things out.'

'Is there – anything I can do to help Grant?'

He turned towards her eagerly. 'As a matter of fact there probably is. Let's drink our coffee then go for a walk and I can tell you what the problem is. I can't talk about it here,' he indicated the other tables around them, 'it's too personal and upsetting.'

She finished her coffee quickly. 'I don't want to be too long Grant,' she said gently. 'I'll listen of course, but I have plans of my own you see.'

'It won't take long Cathy. If you're ready, let's go now.' As she stood up she saw Scott and he wasn't alone. Walking by his side and deep in conversation with him was the golden haired girl from the gondola. It was hard to concentrate on the tale Grant was telling her after that, but she tried. He was hesitant at first, saying he didn't quite know where to start and she needed to understand something about his family background first. Then he launched into a story about his father's two marriages, and she suddenly said, quite briskly, 'Grant, get to the point *please*. I do have to get back in reasonable time.'

They were in an alley by then, somewhere she didn't recognise. The small canal looked murky and the tall apartments on each side seemed sinister and menacing, blocking out the morning sun and casting eerie shadows.

Grant had his arm linked through hers now, and he gripped her tightly as he hurried her on and said, 'While I was away I realised how much you've come to mean to me during this last few months, and...' he glanced quickly over his shoulder and at that moment two men who were standing in the dappled shadows as they drew level reached out and forcibly bundled her inside the building. One had his hand firmly across her mouth as they rushed her up the stone staircase, higher and higher, faster and faster. She struggled, but her strength counted for nothing against the two of them.

They pushed her into a small room and onto a chair. One still kept his hand over her mouth, while the other produced a long, wide strip of sheeting and securely tied it round to prevent anything except muffled sounds coming through.

'Keep still and quiet and no harm will come to you,' one of them said. He moved deftly out of the way as she lashed at him with her foot. 'You've asked for it.' His dark eyes blazed at her, and going to the corner of the almost bare room, he picked up some thick rope lying there. 'I hoped not to have to tie you up, Signorina, but your attitude forces me to. However I will not cut too deeply into that delicate skin – only enough to prevent you from damaging us.'

She fought as they tied her up, securing her to the chair in two places, around her waist and then across her lap, tethering the rope beneath the seat of the chair.

'That's better, now we can talk. No, not you Signorina,' something like a smile flitted briefly across his features. 'We will do the talking, and later, when you have settled down we will remove the bandages from your lips and give you a drink.'

His tone changed from velvety sarcasm to brutal reality. 'We shall hold you ransom and when we have the money you will be free – and unharmed if you behave yourself. I have your aunt's jewels here, and on payment of the money we could have raised on those, then you will go free. Giorgio, take the note. I will handle the girl.'

Frightened now, Cathy wondered where Grant was. Had they captured him too, or when he saw what was happening had he escaped and was even now raising the alarm? As the one called Giorgio disappeared from her view and she heard him clattering down the stairs a ray of hope surged through her. Now they were one to one. If she could only get her legs free she could surely kick him sufficiently to double him up long enough for her to escape.

He walked towards the window and gazed silently down until her attempts to scream brought him back to her. 'If you persist in this foolishness I shall have to draw the gag tighter,' he said. 'It is your own fault you are bound like this, had you been reasonable you could have enjoyed greater freedom.' He walked round the back of the chair and checked the tightness of all her bonds and she knew she could not get away except by a fluke. Her only hope was Grant. Where was he? If only she hadn't tried to scream she would have her voice free now. Frantically she tried to explain that she would behave if he would release the gag round her face, but with arms and legs tied she could not point, but only mumble incoherently through the sheeting and try to make him see what she was saying by the expression in her eyes.

'Keep quiet,' he said sharply, and she too heard footsteps running up the stone stairs. Giorgio burst quickly into the room. 'Everything OK?' her guard asked.

'Yes.'

'The girl wants the gag off I think. Got your gun?'

'Yes Paolo.' He reached into his hip pocket and slid out a pistol. The one called Paolo moved closer.

'Any tricks and we use it,' he said, 'Giorgio is a crack shot. If you scream it's the end for you. If you behave we shall not hurt you.' He walked behind her chair and untied the sheeting while Giorgio kept the gun trained on her.

Chapter 14

Cathy did not scream. She dare not risk the menace of that gun. He could be bluffing but she wasn't about to find out. They gave her a drink of orange from a half full bottle. She tried to ask them about Grant, but they looked warily at each other and at her.

'The man I was with, what have you done with him?' she said. Giorgio spat noisily on the floor. 'He ran away.'

Her spirits soared for surely by now he had alerted Mary and Scott. Yes indeed, Scott, Guy, Betty, and half the Italian Polizia were looking for them now. And Grant of course could lead them straight here... that is odd, she thought – they must realise he will raise the alarm. Perhaps they have him too. Maybe others of the gang went after him when he ran, and now have him holed up somewhere as well. She tried to find out more, but Paolo threatened the return of the gag if she persisted in talking too much.

'I will tell you all you need to know, Signorina. Your policeman friend has made it,' he paused as he searched for the right word, although his English was excellent, 'difficult, for us to sell your aunt's jewellery. So we now have you. They will pay well for your return and you take the baubles with you for they are no use to us if we cannot sell them.'

'I see,' she murmured, not knowing whether to bless or curse Scott for this latest predicament. Hardly his fault of course. He could not have known they would kidnap her in lieu of the jewels. There was one ray of hope. If they hadn't caught Grant, or caught up with him, he could not only alert the police but lead them to her.

Even as the thoughts formulated in her mind she dismissed them. They had caught him of course. That was why they weren't bothered about moving from this place. She knew she could not rely on Grant's escape to alert Mary and Scott to where she was. But why hadn't they brought him back here?

'You want something to eat?' Paolo, who seemed to be the 'boss' asked her. 'It will probably be several hours before we have the money and you are released.'

'What if they cannot pay?' she asked simply.

He put a finger to his throat and drew it quickly across, 'Then you and the baubles will never be seen again.' Cathy shivered.

'You want something to eat?' Paolo repeated.

'Might as well,' she said faintly, 'it looks as if I'm stuck here with you for some time.'

'That is better.' Paolo actually smiled at her. 'We have plenty of food and if you behave we shall treat you well. Try any tricks and –'once more he made the theatrical gesture of the knife across the throat.

'I've got the message,' Cathy said slowly. Slowly because she wanted him to think that she was cooler than she really was, and also because it gave her time to think. She was silent when Giorgio gave Paolo the gun and went out of the room, presumably to fetch the promised meal. She watched Paolo relax. That was the answer, she thought, to let him, to let both of them, think she had accepted the situation, and possibly there would be a

157

chance for her to escape. It didn't look likely now, but if she kept her wits about her and tried to make friends with them...

The next few hours seemed like a bad dream to Cathy. When Giorgio returned with a tray containing three giant rolls filled with salami, a large bottle of red wine and three glasses she knew beyond doubt that Grant had not escaped. They surely would not be so confident if he had.

Paolo handed the gun back to Giorgio, then came and untied her bonds himself. 'You cannot escape from here,' he said, 'we are very high up and there is nobody in the building but us. If you scream or make a false move you know what will happen.' He pointed to Giorgio who had put the gun back into his pocket, but who now patted it reassuringly.

'How long do you think it will be?' she asked boldly. Paolo shrugged his massive shoulders, 'Who knows?'

She almost mentioned Grant again, and then had second thoughts. She did not want to draw unnecessary attention to him. It was obvious that they had him captive too, maybe even in this very building, but Paolo and Giorgio were definitely in charge of her. She wondered how many there were altogether in this gang and who the leader was. Not Paolo. Cathy thought he was simply the senior of the two guarding her. Now her arms and legs were free she felt better.

'I didn't think I would be hungry,' she said carefully, 'yet I find I am. May I wash my hands though before I eat?'

They exchanged wary looks and Paolo said, 'I will take you to the bathroom and wait outside. You will have exactly two minutes and if you are not out by then I shall come in.' Cathy shivered again, realising that there was very little chance of her outwitting them on her own.

The bathroom was on the landing so there was no opportunity of seeing more of the layout of the building she was in. They searched her first.

'Whatever for?' she asked in exasperation, 'I have no rope to escape with, and anyway I've never been good with heights.' But this time neither of them smiled.

'We have to be sure you do not try anything, Signorina. Do not lock the door, I can easily blast it open,' he indicated the gun which he had taken back from Giorgio.

She was no longer than the two minutes, and in the quick look at the high window, which she had to stand on the toilet seat to reach, she knew it was hopeless to attract attention from so great a distance. The only possible way was with a note flung down and hopefully picked up by someone responsible enough to take it to the right quarters. That was an unlikely chance, and they had been thorough, making sure she had no means of doing this or leaving a lipstick message on the window itself by making her leave her handbag behind.

On returning to the main room Paolo moved a small table from the window to the centre. It was a large room and the only furniture apart from the table and five chairs scattered at intervals around, was an old fashioned bureau with half a dozen books sitting on the lower shelves and some paper and envelopes rammed untidily into the slotted compartments by the desk.

They ate the meal in what seemed to Cathy an almost embarrassed silence. When he went to pour more wine into her glass she stopped him. 'Thank you but I have had enough,' she said. He shrugged his shoulders expressively. 'Suit yourself, Signorina. It passes the time.'

His remark gave her an idea which she admitted to herself was a bit far-fetched, but, it might work. Worth a try anyway. If she could get them both so drunk that they fell asleep… not likely she repeated to herself to stem the excitement the thought of freedom and safety again after these few hours brought her. They may find it boring just waiting for a reply to their ransom note, but they seemed experienced enough to have the patience to carry it through. After pouring them both another glassful Paolo pushed the stopper firmly in.

'You clear away, Giorgio. I will guard the girl,' he said. When Giorgio returned from the kitchen she and Paolo had not spoken more than a few words. Each time she tried he answered briefly and in a tone which left her in no doubt that he was not prepared to turn this into a friendly *we will get to know* each other episode. She glanced towards her wrist to look at her watch and suddenly the gun was within inches of her face.

'I do not wish to shoot such a beautiful Signorina.' Paola's grim voice spoke, and his hand was steady on the deadly weapon he was holding, 'but sudden movements can be misconstrued. You wanted to know the time? You should have asked. Do not do that again.'

He lowered the gun and moved away from her and as he did so her enormous calm broke and she felt a clammy perspiration flowing from her hair, down her cheeks, onto her neck, and into the crevices of her breasts. She heard a voice, was it Paolo's or Giorgio's, saying, "Quick, catch her,' and the next thing she focused was a pair of deep, dark eyes gazing into hers.

'That is better, Signorina.' It was Giorgio, and his voice was quiet, almost gentle, yet she detected that firmness that, even feeling as weak as she did now, she knew would allow no mercy.

'What happened?' she asked him. He drew back a little, but kept hold of her hands. 'You fainted. Very theatrical it was. Suddenly went white as a clown and – pff– Paolo catch you.'

She struggled to sit up and he helped her. She was on the floor and he said quietly, 'Paolo is making you some English tea.'

As Giorgio helped her onto her feet and into the chair again Paolo came in with some mugs of watery tea. Did he look anxious? She couldn't be sure, but a plan formed in her mind at that moment. She would not faint again – that anyway had been genuine, the shock of the gun so close it was almost jabbing into her, but she would pretend a weakness. The plan extended itself even as it formed. She would not make it a feminine swooning at the pressure sort of thing, they were obviously both intelligent men, but she would plead a weak heart, really lay it on thick.

They both spoke and understood English so well she must be careful to get it right. 'Thank you,' she murmured quietly as Paolo handed her a mug of tea. 'Good, I'm glad you made it weak – I'm not allowed anything too strong.' She warmed to her theme, 'I should not have had the wine really, but I thought it wouldn't hurt just once.'

She watched them, trying by her expression to convey enough apprehension over her health to be worried by what had happened, yet not give too much away.

'Why?' Paolo's voice was sharp and she saw his hand resting on the gun in his pocket.

'I have a heart condition. Nothing to worry about, except, except under stress.' She hurried quickly on, 'I'm all right now so don't worry about it, but please, no sudden shocks.'

'Drink the tea.' he said. A few minutes later he whispered something to Giorgio, then gave him the gun. As he passed her chair he said, 'No tricks.'

Giorgio proved a better conversationalist than Paolo. His English wasn't the excellent standard of his colleague, but it was fluent nevertheless, and he seemed more inclined to talk. She tried to phrase her questions into statements, saying, 'Of course you know my aunt will not be able to raise any money without the jewels.'

'You will take the jewels with you,' he replied.

'But she'll need them first if she is to get money together.'

'Do not question, Signorina,' he said quite firmly, 'the note explains she will have the gems returned.'

'But Giorgio...'

'No. I must not talk with you. You will please be silent.'

She sighed exaggeratedly and closed her eyes for a few seconds. When she opened them Giorgio was regarding her intently, although he looked away when he saw she was fully awake.

'I get terribly stiff,' she said, 'I really need to walk around a bit to let the blood circulate properly.'

'You sit still. His hand fingered the gun in his pocket

'I have no choice Giorgio,' she said weakly, 'but surely it wouldn't hurt to let me move about. You could lock the door if it makes you feel better – safer,' she amended, beginning to enjoy herself, for she had seen that it was almost one o'clock and by now the search for her and Grant would surely be under way. Surely it would include a search of empty properties like this one, and although Giorgio and Paolo had a gun between them the polizia would be superiorly equipped. She trembled as she realised again the very great danger she was in. Not only herself but Grant also, for she knew within herself that he too was held prisoner somewhere. They would never had let him escape and raise the alarm.

'Very well, Signorina, when Paolo returns I will talk to him and possibly we will allow you to walk about a little and stretch your legs. Until then you must stay sitting down and no harm will come to you. We do not wish to hurt you, you understand, his dark eyes gazing at her earnestly and rather warmly.

163

'Of course I do.' She answered. I know you are simply doing your job, that someone higher than you is actually giving the orders. But I think you will have to be practical about all this, Giorgio,' she deliberately used his name, 'because the longer you hold me here the more worried I shall become and I can't help my condition. Well I don't need to point that out to you. I can tell you understand.' She was quiet for several minutes, and then she asked him what the note to her aunt said.

'I cannot tell you.'

'Or maybe you don't know,' she suggested, her voice softly appealing. 'How many does the money have to be divided between Giorgio? Because we are not a rich family. It is one thing to steal my aunt's jewellery and sell it, but to hold me ransom… I'm afraid the whole family clubbing together would not be able to raise that kind of money.'

Giorgio didn't answer and she was busy working out what to say next to persuade him to her side when the sound of footsteps running up the stairs halted her. Paolo entered and came quickly across the room to Giorgio's side, saying something to him in Italian. Giorgio looked across to her and answered rapidly, again in Italian.

In the few months she had lived here Cathy had picked up a little of the language, but not much because so many of Mary's friends were English. She guessed that Giorgio was telling Paolo that she wanted to walk about the room. From his facial expressions and his hand gestures she saw that he was pleading her case, or so it seemed, but Paolo wasn't having any. After a few moments he came towards her.

'No. You are all right. There is nothing wrong with your heart,' he said, 'do not try to make a fool of Paolo.' Then he reverted to his native language, and at a vast speed, to Giorgio.

A feeling of depression settled in Cathy. For half an hour there she had hoped, really hoped, and almost believed that she could get at least one of them on her side, or so sympathetic to her cause that he would not obstruct if she had a chance of escape, but it was obvious that Paolo was in charge here. He came over to her again now.

'You stay where you are. I will not have you walking about the room, and no more questions. You only speak when spoken to. Now listen to me, the boss says it may take longer than we think and we must be ready to move quickly if necessary. If this proves so,' he paused dramatically after his long drawn out words, 'then you will obey immediately or else.' And he again drew his hand across his throat, then took a pretend gun from his pocket and playacted a shooting. 'Do you understand, Signorina?' She nodded. 'Good. Then if I have to pull the trigger – if you force me to do so, I shall not have a guilty conscious because, as you say in your country, you know the score.'

They all settled into an uncomfortable silence. If she had won the previous round with Giorgio she had definitely lost this one with Paolo, and he was the boss here, although there was obviously a greater and higher

165

one, the one he had referred to, the one Scott had been convinced about from the beginning.

'Someone is masterminding this gang.' His voice seemed so close, his presence so near. Oh Scott, she moaned within herself, I wish I knew what was happening now, what you and Mary and Betty and Guy are doing... Then I would have a better idea of how to behave, how to get out of this. She tried to picture them, and almost looked at her watch, then, remembering the last time she had done this she thought better of it and asked Paolo the time.

'You may look,' he said. Her watch registered a quarter to three. She had arranged to meet Scott at two, and tears filled her eyes now as she recalled their date. Why, oh why hadn't she said yes to the all day trip he had planned? Her thoughts flashed to Grant and she wondered again what they had done with him. They must have caught him when he ran. Was he here, in a downstairs room, or being held somewhere else? And who was his guard? Another member of the gang or the boss himself? In spite of the heat she went suddenly cold as she wondered if they had killed him.

She twisted her ankles round each other and saw Paolo's expression change. 'I'm stiff,' she said by way of explanation, and still hoping to exploit the now very slight advantage she had gained when she had fainted. He nodded towards her but was silent and she tried to think how Scott would tackle the situation she found herself in.

Thoughts of Scott almost brought the tears to her eyes, but she kept them at bay and busied her mind with trying to form a plan for escape should the slightest opportunity arise. The greatest danger was from that gun of course, or the knife, which she had not so far seen, but which Paolo seemed to enjoy dramatising for her. She did not doubt that he had one. If she could not see any immediate means of escape perhaps she could find out the name of the boss he talked of. She felt colour surge into her cheeks as she visualised herself telling Scott his name and where he could be located when she was released from this prison. He would be pleased. More than that – why he would be thrilled and … she was so engrossed that she did not hear the footsteps coming up the stairs, but Paolo and Giorgio did, and it was the alarm in their faces that jerked her violently from the imagined future to the present.

Paolo reached the door in a few long strides, and a hurried, almost panicky conversation took place. She couldn't hear it all, but enough words reached her to know that Scott was gaining on them and possibly knew where they were. Paolo closed the door and said sharply to Giorgio, 'Take the gun and the girl.' He glanced rapidly round the room, then, his dark eyes intent on her face, 'We are moving to another apartment. The gun will be at your back all the time. If you make, or even seem to make one false move, Giorgio will use it. Do you understand?'

She felt herself nodding her head, although she made no conscious decision to do so. They left the building together, looking, she realised like three friends out for a stroll.

'We do not go too quickly,' Paolo told them, 'we do nothing, absolutely nothing to excite curiosity or speculation.'

The new building wasn't far. It took them perhaps five minutes to walk to it through several narrow alleyways, and they did not pass more than two people. Not that it would have made much difference, she thought bitterly, if they had walked across San Marco itself, because, with the hard nozzle of the gun pressing into her back as she went, and Paolo and Giorgio holding an arm and hand each. She realised they looked more like friends or lovers than predators and victim.

Chapter 15

The apartment they took her to was again at the top of the building. This one was fully furnished and looked lived in. Italian books and papers were stacked on the table and there were several ashtrays around the room, which was small and rather dark. She noticed at once that it also had a telephone. If only she had a chance, but she knew that was unlikely, yet it provided her with the first sign of hope so far.

'Sit there,' Paolo said, pushing her roughly into a brown covered armchair, 'and remember Giorgo has you covered.'

Well at least she wasn't tied up this time. She sat stiffly upright in the rather hard armchair and decided to play up her 'heart condition.' It was odd but they would have no compunctions about shooting her, or even knifing her she thought, but seemed wary about letting her die by natural causes. Or perhaps they thought that with such a condition she would not die, but become ill, too ill to hold prisoner or run from one building to another with. I will bide my time, she thought, there is hope yet.

While Giorgio pulled up a straight-backed chair and sat facing her, Paolo walked round the tiny room. She watched him until he moved towards the window and out of her vision. She knew better now than to swivel round after him. The first shock of that gun poking into her face had genuinely made her faint. Now she was used to seeing it, but she did not underestimate the lengths these two would go, and she didn't want to die this way.

She didn't want to die at all, not for ages and ages yet. There was all her living still to do. With Scott. The memory of his voice telling her he was in love with her sent the blood coursing hotly through her veins. Was it really only last night?

The sound of the telephone ringing cut into her thoughts, and Paolo answered it briskly and in Italian. 'Si, si.' The rest was, to her, just a gabble. If only he would talk slower she might understand a little of it. After the conversation he walked over to Giorgio and spoke to him softly, but again in Italian. Cathy tried to gauge by their expressions whether it was good news for them or for her, but it was impossible.

'What is happening please?' she asked Paolo

'You will find out. You will be released when we get the money.'

'How long?'

'No more questions.' Once again he ran his finger across his throat, and then he turned to Giorgio. 'Go and check the boat is ready,' he instructed, 'give me the gun.'

Giorgio had only been gone a short while when the telephone rang again. Paolo grasped her wrist and pulled her from the chair. 'Remember this,' he said, jabbing the gun against her body, 'come.' Together they went to answer the telephone. He picked the receiver up with his left hand, keeping the gun in his right, and all the time she could feel its menace and knew his finger was at the ready. Briefly she wondered if she could possibly kick it away, but dismissed the idea. Yet there must be something she could do while they were one to one. The conversation this time was extremely short. All Paolo said was 'Si' at the end of what must have been fresh directions from the boss.

She was so frustrated at not being able to discover anything further, or do anything to help her situation that she forgot to be frightened and, as Paolo marched her back to the chair and started to jerk her into it she stiffened and glared defiantly at him.

'I need to stand, to stretch my legs,' she said.

'You will sit,' he thundered, his black brows frowning together so they almost joined forces. He pushed her violently into the chair.

Gasping as much with anger as with his treatment of her she withdrew into her thoughts. Giorgio had been told to get the boat ready, so did that mean they were going o release her? Would they take her back to Mary's by boat? It was possible, she supposed, but risky from their point of view surely. They could push her out onto the landing stage and get away but she could alert other craft already in the water.

No, they were going to use the boat to transport her somewhere else. So did that mean that Scott and the police were getting nearer? Suddenly she knew what she had to do. Leave a clue here, preferably something that would help them to know quickly where she had now been taken. The first thing was obvious – she must leave something of hers so they would know she had been here. If only she could scribble a note. She had a pen and small notebook in her handbag if she could get hold of it. She could drop her handkerchief as they went out, which she felt sure now they would soon be doing.

'May I have my handbag please?' she said, 'I need my handkerchief.' She sneezed as realistically as she could manage. Keeping the gun aimed in her direction Paolo took the bag from the sideboard, opened it and gave her the small embroidered hankie. He had allowed her to carry the bag when they came from one apartment to the other, and had taken it from her immediately on their arrival here. She took the handkerchief from him slowly, calmly. 'Thank you,' she said, and opening it out she put it to her nose and faked another couple of sneezes. Mustn't overdo it, she thought, so after a vigorous blow and wipe she rolled the tiny scrap of a handkerchief up and tucked it into the short elasticated sleeve of her dress.

Now how could she leave information? The lipstick was in her bag, but wily Paolo was never going to let her have that. Still she had the handkerchief, and as long as they didn't see what she did with it, perhaps she could twist it into the shape of a boat. Yes, that was it. Ask to go to the bathroom and manipulate the handkerchief o look like a boat to leave as a clue, both to the fact that she had been here and the means by which she left.

Carried away now with her ideas she wondered if, as this place was someone's home and not empty like the first hideout, there might be some useful tools in a bathroom cabinet.

'Paolo, I need to…' but even as she was speaking two things happened. Giorgio returned and the telephone rang again. Paolo gave Giorgio the gun and strode quickly over to the instrument. This time he spoke in English.

'Yes.' A pause, then, 'Yes, yes. I understand. To your place. Right.'

Giorgio had already pulled her from the chair, but, in spite of the gun this time she said angrily, 'I can manage by myself, stop manhandling me.'

'Be quiet.' It was Paolo, not Giorgio who answered. 'We are leaving here in a moment. The same procedure as before. You will come quickly with us down the stairs and after that you will behave normally. And remember the gun is loaded.'

He led the way, saying to Giorgio, 'I will start the engine. Come quickly now.' Then he ran the rest of the way down the stairs and she and Giorgio followed at a smart, but more reasonable pace. She managed to take the handkerchief from her sleeve and leave it on the chair where it would be sure to be seen, but alas for her ideas of having it in the shape of a boat.

Giorgio closed the door and with his gun poking into her ribs under the pretence of Giorgio's arm around her, she had no alternative but to go along with him. They hurried along the alley, and there, on a small, dirty canal, was a motorboat with its engine running. As soon as they were on board Paolo cast off and the small craft shot through the murky water.

Surely, she thought, there would be an opportunity now they were out in the open, to escape or attract someone's attention to the gang. The touch of the gun through her thin dress, under cover of Giorgio's arm around her, squashed the idea rapidly. But when they disembarked at their new destination she must be ready, for Paolo would need to secure the boat and if she could only distract Giorgio for a few seconds …

Her chance came sooner than she expected. Paolo, swerving to avoid another boat as he left the smaller waters and entered the Grand Canal, bumped them closer together and she felt the gun move slightly.

'Please,' she whispered to Giorgio, feeling his excitement as his hand brushed against her breast, 'I couldn't get out if I tried with all this traffic around and I'm frightened.' She wriggled even closer and he laid the gun between them and put his arm round her waist.

'It would be foolish,' he agreed, 'if you were not mown down you would not be able to swim far in the canal waters.' His hand moved downwards and she kept perfectly still as she felt his excitement throbbing next to her.

Paolo, who had slowed his speed amongst the many and varied styles of craft in the main canal, swung out into the Adriatic as they approached San Marco.

'Check that no-one is following us,' he ordered, and Giorgio turned quickly round to see.

In those two seconds Cathy took the gun and dropped it over the side. As she did so Giorgio's voice covered the splash as he shouted, 'Two men in a boat – one of them is Scott Underwood.'

Her heart seemed to soar with the impetus of the craft as Paolo directed it towards the islands. She dare not look round herself. She knew that Giorgio had not yet realised the gun was overboard, but it was only a matter of time, and they still had her, and presumably the knife Paolo had warned her about so often during these last few incredible hours. Yet the knowledge that Scott was close filled her with elation. Whatever happened now, wherever they took her, he would see, and eventually rescue her.

As Giorgio turned back he felt for the gun, then looked at her wildly and she knew he thought she had it concealed about her person. Well, so much better, except that it would not take him long to realise what she had done when she didn't produce it.

'How close is he?' This came from Paolo, who seemed now to be exceeding all speed limits, if there were any in operation on the canal, she thought.

'A few yards.'

'When we are nearing the island, shoot. I'll slow down then.'

Cathy's heart lurched sickeningly. Thank God she had the opportunity and thank God she took it. Scott wouldn't stand much chance if, as Paolo had said Giorgio was a crack shot. She knew that Scott wasn't armed.

They were well away from the mainstream of traffic now. There were boats out here, but more spread out, and now they were heading for one of the islands – she had no idea which. She still had not dared to turn round so did not know who the second person in the boat with

Scott was. Not a policeman or Giorgio would surely have mentioned it. She suspected it was Grant or Guy and that it was Guy's boat that was pursuing them so closely that she could hear the throbbing of their engine now as well as Paolo's. As the island loomed closer Paolio slowed down and called out in Italian.

'I can't,' Giorgio answered, 'the gun has gone.'

'Fool. Fool. Imbecile.'

The boat roared onto the island and Paolo leapt from it and as Cathy made to dodge him, he grabbed hold of the skirt of her dress, ripping the cotton material as he did so. He caught her quickly and held her arm in a vicelike grip – his other hand was clutching Mary's jewellery box.

She heard the crunch of the pursuing craft and made a wild lunge to take the box from him. He shouted something in Italian as her long fingernails scratched his bare arms. He had her on the ground as Scott pounded up to them and, throwing the jewel box down too he whipped out a knife and held it to her throat.

'You come one step nearer and I use it on the girl.'

Cathy was more frightened now than she had ever been in her life. They seemed to be the only people on the island and now, because of her stupidity in believing that she could get the box from him she had jeopardised everything, even her own life. She could see the shining blade glinting in the hot sun, only inches away from her throat, and in the distance she heard the scuffling of a fight. Guy, or Grant and Giorgio, it must be because Scott was standing right there. She could see his feet in brown sandals and the sight made her want to cry. The scuffling stopped and Paolo's voice was sharp with anxiety again as he said, 'You too, do not come any closer or the girl gets it.'

Slowly he moved the knife across the distance of her throat. 'One false move and…' he swished it quickly and, although it was inches away she gasped out loud.

'All right.' She could still see Scott's feet, perfectly still near where she was half laying and half propped on her elbow.

'All I want is the girl. Let me take the girl and I'll go.'

'She's my protection,' Paolo said.

'The boss told you not to harm her – I heard him. It won't only be us you'll have to fear if that knife slips…'

Cathy had read in thrillers about someone's blood running cold. At that moment she couldn't feel any blood in her veins at all. In spite of the brilliant sunshine she was icy cold.

'You have a chance to get away if you go now,' Scott said. 'The polizia have the boss, but they don't know I'm here. If you give me that knife, or at least put it away and get into your boat, no-one will chase you until, or unless the boss grasses. Do you understand what I am saying? I'm giving you the chance of freedom. The game is up for the gang, but you two can still escape if you choose – but not with murder.'

The silence was awful. Cathy was afraid that she would move and that would be the end, for the face hovering over her was tense with fear, yet it didn't panic. Paolo was strong, if he had been in the back of the boat with her instead of Giorgio she knew she would not have had a chance to throw the gun overboard. He would never have succumbed to such age-old wiles as Giorgio had.

Suddenly the ordeal was over. The silver gleam of the knife moved. She was too paralytic to even scream. She could still see Scott's feet, encased in their sandals but not moving, but the knife had gone from her throat. The next thing she was conscious of was the sound of the motorboat, and the next that Scott was bending over her, his arms cradling her as though she were a child, a very precious child.

'Cathy, oh Cathy.'

'Scott.' She tried to think. 'Shouldn't – sh - - shouldn't you be going after them?'

A tear splashed onto her face and he didn't reply. Then he picked her up into his arms and carried her over to the boat.

'You all right, Guy?'

'Yes. A bit bruised but he's in a worse state than I am.' He too climbed into the boat.

'I'm taking you back to Mary,' Scott said, in control of his emotions again now, 'then I have to round up the gang.' He started the motor and less than fifteen minutes later they were at Casa Ristori and he was helping her onto the landing stage.

'Sure you are OK, Cathy?' he said.

'I'm fine now.'

'I won't come up then. Mary and Betty are there and I'll be back later.'

'Be careful,' Guy said.

Cathy found her voice, 'Where are you going?'

'I have to find *the boss*. I lied. He is still free. The polizia can pick the others up some time, but I need the brains behind the organisation, and I think I know where to find him.'

Cathy and Guy went up in the lift, and Mary and Betty, who heard it ascending, were waiting as it reached the landing.

Chapter 16

'We recovered the jewels,' Cathy told Mary when the emotion of those first moments was over and Ginette had been despatched to the kitchen to fetch long cool drinks.

'Damn the jewels. All that really matters is that you are safe. You and Scott. And Grant,' she added, seemingly as an afterthought. She gazed around the room as though expecting him to appear.

'Where did Grant go?' she asked Betty. Betty glanced round too. 'Don't know Mary. I thought he was following us when we heard the lift. May be in the loo.'

'You mean – Grant's here?' Cathy asked breathlessly.

'Well he was a few moments ago. Hey, I suppose he is still in the building? Suppose they were waiting downstairs and came up for him when they saw that Cathy was back?'

Mary rose and hurried to the door, calling his name. They heard her go to the kitchen, speak to Ginette, and then a few seconds later she re-entered the room to say, 'He isn't here – not in the bathroom, nor the bedrooms. Oh my God, do you think they were hovering around downstairs all the time?'

'Please,' Cathy said, 'will you tell me what you're talking about? Surely if – if the gang have got Grant we should be doing something about it?'

'What can we do?' Betty said, 'we haven't a clue as to who they are, or where they may have taken him.'

At Mary's suggestion they went downstairs to the little piazza at the back of the apartment and, if there was anyone about, ask them if they had seen him.

There were a couple of people sitting at one of the tables outside the café, but when questioned they said that they had only just arrived there and had not noticed anybody leaving the apartment opposite nor seen anything strange happening in the square. They returned to the flat and Cathy walked towards the window and gazed onto the canal far, far below.

'Tell me about Grant,' she said, 'how he came to be here, because the last I saw of him was when these two men grabbed me when Grant and I were walking together. I thought at first that he had escaped and alerted you, and then I thought that he too must have been caught and held somewhere else.'

'Don't worry too much,' Betty said gently, 'Scot will probably find him. Or the polizia will. Tell us, if you feel up to it dear, about what happened to you.'

So Cathy launched into her story, finishing with the chase to the seemingly uninhabited island. She only omitted Scott's tears when he had her safely in his arms. She had not fully taken in the wonder of that herself yet, and anyway it was such a private moment.

Then they told her how, after Scott and Guy had left in the boat, Grant arrived. 'He rang the bell and I rushed down to let him in. At first I thought it was Scott back and that he had forgotten something he needed,' she said, 'because it happened within minutes of him going.'

'And what did Grant say. What did he tell you?'

'That two men had jumped out from an alleyway and kidnapped you.'

'He gave us a note,' Mary said slowly, 'from the kidnappers. He was in a bit of a state emotionally. Apparently when he saw that he couldn't rescue you himself he ran to fetch help, but two more of the gang caught up with him and threatened him with knives, he said. They took him into the house, kept him tied up for hours, and then they wrote out a ransom note and forced him to bring it here to me.'

'How long ago was this Mary?'

'About – he had been here about ten minutes when you arrived I should think. We had already had two ransom telephone calls you see, and been warned that if we contacted the police we would not see you again.' Mary's voice broke. 'I said – that I would have to get some money from the bank and had in fact arranged to meet one of the – one of the bandits at the bank tomorrow. But I said that without the jewellery I couldn't raise the money and he – he was going to bring the jewels so I could use them as security. It was terrible,' she said, suddenly covering her face with her hands to hide her tears. 'He described what would happen to you if I so much as gave a hint to anyone.'

Betty went to her and Cathy said quietly, 'Don't talk about it if you'd rather not. What a blessing Betty and Guy were here too, so they knew.'

'Yes.' Mary looked up and wiped her eyes, 'sorry about that. When Scott arrived out of the blue and said he was taking Guy's boat because he had them on the run, we didn't know if you were with them or not.'

Guy took up the tale, 'I said I'd go with them – two pair of hands are better than one if it comes to fisticuffs I reckon, and he was dealing with a bunch of desperate men.'

'I see,' Cathy said, 'so after you and Scott had gone, Grant arrived here.'

'That's right,' Mary chimed in again, 'he said you were tied up and they planned to move you tonight but if we gave the money now, or even some of it, they would not harm either of you. He said they were waiting outside for him and that if anyone telephoned the police you would be the first...'

Guy looked at the clock. 'I should have gone with Scott,' he said, 'we don't even know where he was making for.'

He looked through the window, 'He has taken the boat, but from what little he said I don't believe he was heading back to the islands and yet he seemed confident that he knew where to go. Cathy, could you direct us to the place where you were held captive, do you think?'

She shook her head. 'I didn't take a lot of notice. I wish I had. I met Grant at Academia, we had a coffee and then I think we walked about half a mile. It was quiet, a back street really.'

'Never mind, that's a help. It gives us a district. And the police know where he is going I believe. He told me in the boat just before the chase that they had been alerted.'

Cathy sat quietly while the rest of them talked and offered possibilities, knowing that the only thing they could successfully do without interfering with police procedure, was to wait. She hoped Grant was all right and she prayed that Scott was.

When the telephone rang they jumped and Guy offered to answer it. They all felt the anti-climax when he came back into the room to say it was one of Mary's friends and not information from anyone about what was happening.

Cathy looked at her watch and saw it was almost eight o'clock. Outside the lovely special sort of Venetian evening light was bathing the canal in romance. Restlessly she rose and once again went to gaze through the window. Scott must be safe, he must, he must. If anything happens to him I'll never forgive myself, she thought. The memory of the love and concern that had been in his eyes when Paolo removed the knife from the throat she was sure would stay with her forever.

Far, far below she saw the boats and gondolas plying their trade, the colourful skirts and dresses of the holidaying population as they swished and sauntered along on the opposite side, the dark, plain colours of the older Italians out for an evening stroll, the chic of the younger ones, all looking like distant extras on a film set. Suddenly she saw a boat approaching the landing stage. Was it – yes, yes, it was Scott.

'He's here,' she cried out, 'Scott's just coming in.'

They were in the hall within seconds, waiting impatiently for the lift to rise. She heard the door clang shut and the whir of the machinery, and she felt such an agonising sense of relief that she was almost sick on the spot.

'Hey,' he said, 'I didn't expect a reception committee.'

'Scott, your eye,' she whispered, gazing at the bruises forming above and beneath his right eye.

'It probably looks worse than it is,' he replied, leading the way back into the drawing room. I'll tell you about it in a moment. Right now I need some strong coffee I think.'

Ginette, who had come from the kitchen on hearing the commotion, quickly ran back, saying, 'Five minutes and coffee will be in. I get you something to eat too?'

He grinned, then grimaced as it hurt his wounded face, 'No thanks, just lots and lots of coffee.'

'Should we bathe that eye, Scott?' It was Betty who spoke, 'It looks pretty nasty.'

'It's OK. Don't fuss please,' he said, 'bit tender that's all.'

When he was comfortably settled Cathy sat on the floor by his chair and his hand crept down and gently rested across her shoulders.

'Is Grant all right?' she said, 'where is he?'

She couldn't fathom the expression on his face, and she felt his hands move gently across her back, then he said slowly, 'you can't be serious, Cathy.'

'But of course I am.' Surely, she thought, we aren't going to quarrel over Grant Taggart now?

185

'He's behind bars where he should be.' he said grimly, 'you aren't really concerned about him, are you? The Grant Taggarts of the world look after themselves, Cathy.'

She twisted herself round so she was facing him, then turned and gazed at the others who looked as amazed as she felt. 'And at last we have him and most of the gang. The few stragglers will soon be rounded up. In any case without him to lead the thing is broken.'

'But why? What has Grant done?'

Ginette came in with the coffee then and when she had gone Scott stirred his and drank deeply. 'Boy I needed that,' he said.

'What about Grant?'

His fingers dug into her shoulders. 'Grant was the brain behind the gang. The big boss, the one who organised everything. Only this time it all went wrong for him, and at last we have him and most of the gang. The few stragglers will soon be rounded up. In any case, without him to lead the thing is broken.'

'Grant. Grant the leader of a − a gang of thieves. No Scott, you've got the wrong man. Why Grant was here a short while ago, just before we returned, wasn't he?'

She turned to the others for confirmation, and they joined in, echoing her own thoughts that there had somehow or other been a miscarriage of justice, and the real leader was still free. All except Mary, who said quietly, 'There has always been something I couldn't fathom about Grant. When did you know Scott?'

'Only today for sure, but I have suspected for some time. I followed you this morning Cathy, when you went to meet him.'

'You did?' Suddenly she remembered the sighting of him as she and Grant left the café. She remembered who his companion was too. 'I saw you,' she said, and only she knew how much it cost to say this, but, painful as it was it needed to be out in the open now they had committed themselves so deeply. 'You were with a girl.'

'Oh my sister, yes. She flits in and out occasionally. She was here a few weeks ago too but she never stayed long enough to be introduced to anyone, did she Betty?' He smiled across the room to his aunt. 'She's a great girl though and perhaps when we all get back to England she'll stop in one spot a sufficient length of time for you to get acquainted. I didn't realise you saw me, you seemed engrossed in what Taggart was saying to you.'

'And did you follow us then?' she said, disbelief over his revelations regarding Grant, joy over discovering who the gorgeous blonde was, and curiosity as to how far he had followed and how much he had seen, all vying for a place.

'Yes. I sent Barbara back to Betty and Guy's with the message that I thought I had found my quarry. She was due to leave a few hours later anyway, and then I shadowed you. I saw the two men who seized you, but was too late to do anything except dodge out of Taggart's way.'

187

It was like one of Mary's novels unfolding, Cathy thought. That Scott had been so close, had seen so much, was amazing her.

'I contacted the Polizia, then I tried to get into the building where they had taken you, but it was locked. I also had to keep an eye on Taggart of course.'

'What – what did he do Scott, after I had been kidnapped?'

'He went to another apartment not far away, and he was there for some time, then he returned to where you were and let himself in with a key.'

'That must have been when I heard Paolo talking to someone. And the other apartment, the one they took me to afterwards had a telephone, so maybe Grant…, she hesitated, still reluctant to believe that he was the one Giorgio and Paolo had referred to as the boss.

'Yes,' Scott interrupted her, his voice grim, 'I expect he telephoned Mary from there with his dire threats. The one thing he never told you was that he had once been an actor, of sorts, he had many names and more than one voice too.'

Cathy turned towards her aunt. 'You were unsure of him from the start, weren't you?' she said.

'Slightly. I tried not to think he was the ringleader. I – I didn't want him to be actually. I hoped it would turn out to be someone we didn't know.' She laughed nervously, 'But things pointed more and more to it, until today.'

Betty joined in now saying, 'That's right. Today it didn't seem that he could be. Well we thought he had been imprisoned too. We swallowed the whole story, didn't we Mary? About the gangster waiting outside the door for him, about how he tried to rescue you,' she looked across to Cathy, 'I certainly believed him. I suppose if we had managed to rustle up anything like the kind of cash he was after he would have simply disappeared.'

Guy and Scott exchanged glances. 'The most important thing is that you are both safe,' Guy said, 'although slightly wounded,' he added with a grin as he looked at Scott's swollen face.

'And the second good thing,' Scott said, 'is that you have your gems back Mary.'

'Yes. With them of course we could have raised the money.'

'Why couldn't they sell them Scott?' Guy asked, 'Was that something you had a hand in?'

'Yes. Of course they may have found someone who didn't realise but, because we knew the exact contents of the box, we were able to warn all the known fences. We simply made them too hot to handle,' he added grinning and then wincing as the movement hurt his face.

'Grant even went to London when he could see that Rome was a dead duck as far as selling them was concerned. And of course he wanted to get rid of them very quickly, which, in the event, proved difficult.

'So he hit on the idea of kidnapping Cathy and holding her to ransom. When he had the money he may have sent the box back with her – probably would have done because he isn't a fool and he would know that years afterwards we would trace a piece of jewellery if he had hung on and tried to sell then.'

'Cheeky though,' Betty said, 'to come here when he saw you and Guy go off in the boat.'

'Yes, cheeky and clever,' Scott answered. 'If it hadn't been a Sunday and you had been to the bank without telling anyone as he wanted, he would have got away with it, at least briefly. We would have captured him in the end I think, under one of his names.'

It was late when Betty, Guy and Scott finally left. As they reached the door Cathy said, 'Who did that Scott? Paolo or Giorgio or one of these others in the gang?'

'Ah, that little memento has nothing to do with the robbery Cathy, that was a personal score. When Grant was under arrest this evening, he was in the interview still. I had finished with him and turned to leave when he suddenly called my name. Quietly, urgently almost. I turned round – I was only inches away from him in any case, and his fist shot out. I saw stars for a few moments I can tell you, but as I reeled I heard him say, 'The best man won. It's been a fascinating few years Underwood, but that's for having the girl I wanted. That one is for Cathy.'

Chapter 17

Over the next few days Cathy and Scott saw each other as often as possible, because he was flying home at the end of the week. She and Mary would only be a couple of weeks after that. His cheek became a horrible jaundice colour, but he said no permanent damage had been done.

'Has simply spoiled my good looks temporarily, Cathy.' One evening, at Mary's, when Guy and Betty were also present, they talked about the gang. 'The phantom gang you called them at first,' Scott said to Cathy, 'didn't you?'

'Yes. I admit I found it hard to believe there was a plan afoot to steal Mary's jewels. I guess I hadn't realised they were so valuable, or the extent of them. What was more difficult though was your theory that Grant could be involved. You had your suspicions right from the start that he was at the head of it all, didn't you?'

'Mmm, but only suspicions and you cannot condemn a man on those. I had nothing definite to go on at all, at least where he was concerned.'

'Sometimes, even now, it seems incredible,' she said.

'I had the advantage there,' Scott admitted. 'I knew there was a plot to steal the jewels. Well I had heard they were on the agenda, so to speak. And the secretary who took Pippa's place was paid off. There are a few rare people who don't have their price but I've discovered in my job that most of them do.'

'And they put their girl in her place?' Cathy said.

'That's right. And arranged it so that it would be so last minute Mary would take her if she could type and behave reasonably. She was to have liased with Grant in Venice, and would of course have reported Mary's movements, habits, etc.'

'Was she going to steal the jewellery?'

'I'm not sure. I think so. Working from the inside it would have been fairly easy.'

'I suppose so.'

'But fate took a hand,' he went on, 'for not even Taggart could have foreseen that the girl would genuinely fall and break her arm.' He chuckled wickedly. 'That's what threw me when you turned up with Mary the first night I met you. I didn't know about the accident and presumed that you were the new secretary, the one we had our suspicions about…'

'I didn't help by being so recalcitrant did I?' Cathy smiled fondly at him now, 'It seemed to me that you were incredibly nosy and terribly arrogant. Oh Scott, what wrong impressions we sometimes unwittingly give to each other.'

'We certainly got off on the wrong foot, didn't we?' His arm stole round her shoulder and under cover of the older generation's conversation he whispered softly, 'I'm not at all sure that it wasn't that first night that I fell in love with you.'

'I thought you were horrible,' she answered truthfully, 'but that feeling didn't last long.'

'And I thought you were in love with Taggart.'

'Now he's been proved to be a criminal he's Taggart to you, isn't he?' she said, 'before he was Grant.' She wriggled away from him. 'I suppose you find it funny that I was so easily taken in.'

'No Cathy, no I don't, honestly. There were times when I too thought I was mistaken. Yet I couldn't see who else it could be, and anyway I didn't like the fellow because he was sweet on you.'

'For a purpose,' she said bitterly. 'To pump me, and when I think about it he did just that. Oh Scott, the details I must have let slip without realising.'

He replaced his arm round her shoulder and this time she didn't shake it off. 'Looking back,' she said, 'I can see it all, but at the time... he checked with me when the house would be empty, he even invited Mary to his flat the night I went to supper there. Yes, and now I'm thinking about it he made a telephone call that evening which I did think was odd. He explained it by saying it was a business call which could only be done at that time of night. It was quite late.'

'Was that the night the jewels were actually stolen?'

'Yes. It was also the night the gang duffed you up. And all the while I was eating his food and drinking his wine. And providing him with an alibi.'

'You didn't know,' Scott shrugged, 'it was one of those things.'

'I suppose the phone call was to check that everything had gone according to his plans,' she said, 'and that it was safe to bring me home?'

'I expect so. And it had, except that I was there and they had to deal with me as well, which hampered them a bit I imagine.'

'It's like a jigsaw,' she said, 'when it's completed you can see that the bit you didn't think could possibly belong there, does. So many things tie in now, and I was very stupid not to see them before. I guess I was well and truly conned Scott.'

He leaned his head closer to hers so that they touched briefly. 'I truly think that was the only part of the operation he was regretful about Cathy. That it meant something to him to have met you. He really did say not to hurt you to those two thugs. I heard him myself because I was around, just out of sight, for most of the time you were imprisoned. I couldn't see how I could get you out of their clutches, but at least I knew where you were, and knowing how he felt I thought they would treat you reasonably.'

'Gorgio was the best. Nothing much moved Paolo. He was the strong one, the one who would have been brutal eventually.'

'What are you two nattering about?' Mary butted in, 'I'll bet it's about the stolen jewels and the drama we've had this visit.'

'Right first time.' Scott smiled at her. 'We were working out all the intricate details. How,' he hesitated very slightly before saying in a quiet voice, 'Grant knew and tried to get away with yet another robbery. Do you realise Mary that this was the sixteenth the gang had carried out, and although we were aware of them all we hadn't any convincing evidence as to how it was done. Until this time.'

Cathy had a momentary vision of Grant behind bars, then she knew that he deserved it, that in spite of his brief lapse over her, 'you are a bonus' she recalled him saying, he was a thief, a bigtime gangster boss.

'He had started a book,' she said now, 'it was called Pink Elephants.'

'Intriguing title,' Scott said, 'was it any good?'

Mary answered him. 'Yes, actually it was. I read two chapters and the writing was fine. Mind, it had two ingredients that appealed to me, it was a detective story and it was set here in Venice. But Grant had been a journalist at some time during his haphazard career I gather, and he could string words together. It went along at a smart pace. Maybe he'll finish it in jail.'

'Maybe. Or maybe he will plan another coup. By the way, did you ever miss one of the keys to your apartment, Mary?'

'No.'

'How many do you have?'

'Several Scott. Ginette has one, Cathy too. Guy and Betty have one because they are in Venice all the year. I've one in my bag and a couple of spares in the bedroom.'

'In the dressing table drawer, Mary?'

'Yes. In the corner under a pile of handkerchiefs.'

'One of them is missing,' he said slowly, 'the man Maria saw in the bedroom on the night of the party was Grant, and he was looking for the key then. Later, after the excitement was over, he returned and that time he found it. But I was watching, and although I didn't see him go into he bedroom I missed him downstairs and went to look myself.'

He turned to look at Cathy. 'You were so angry with me that night. I believe you thought I was trying to steal the box.'

It was good that they could laugh at the misunderstanding now, she thought as they talked and as more sequences slotted into place.

She and Scott went out for a meal the night before he left for England. 'We'll try for an unobtrusive table, shall we?' he said gingerly touching his cheek. 'One thing, it should be back to normal by the time you return and I meet your mother. Does she know about me by the way?'

'Yes, I wrote to her yesterday.'

The last few weeks in Venice were busy. Mary wanted to finish her book. 'We've had so many distractions this time,' she said. 'I have come to one personal conclusion though.'

'What's that, Mary?'

'I don't believe I could write good detective stories. I think I might become too involved with the people and not enough with the details of the plot. So perhaps romance is my forte after all.'

Cathy laughed, remembering the impressive shelf of her aunt's books back in her London home, and the many jewels which represented a title.

'I think you could write whatever you set your mind on,' she said, 'but maybe, deep down, you prefer the romance.'

There was also a flurry of suppers during the last few days. A goodbye to friends until they either came to London for a visit, or until next year when Mary returned to Venice. Late the night before they left, after returning from an evening spent with Betty and Guy, Cathy opened her window and went outside to stand on her balcony. She wrapped a shawl round her shoulders and hugged it to herself against the chill of the October night. It seemed as though she knew the place so well, as though it could not be her first time here. She had arrived with unhappiness as her companion, but she would be returning with ecstasy.

'We are going to have a wonderful life together,' Scott had said before he left, 'I expect we shall have some marvellous quarrels.' He kissed the tip of her nose when she started to protest. 'Oh but we shall. It wouldn't be you and me if we didn't spark each other off occasionally now, would it? I shall be what you call dictatorial and arrogant, and what I call confident and self-assured,' his cheek touched hers softly, 'and you will be flashing those lovely green eyes and tantalising the frustrated painter in me with that gorgeous chestnut hair…'

Tears of happiness gathered in her eyes as she anticipated tomorrow's journey home, with Scott waiting for her at the end of it, always now and for ever more, waiting and loving.